APR   2021

SARAHLAND

SARAHLAND

STORIES

SAM COHEN

GRAND CENTRAL
PUBLISHING

NEW YORK   BOSTON

Grand Central Publishing
Hachette Book Group
1290 Avenue of the Americas, New York, NY 10104
grandcentralpublishing.com
twitter.com/grandcentralpub

First Edition: March 2021

Grand Central Publishing is a division of Hachette Book Group, Inc. The Grand Central Publishing name and logo is a trademark of Hachette Book Group, Inc.

The publisher is not responsible for websites (or their content) that are not owned by the publisher.

The Hachette Speakers Bureau provides a wide range of authors for speaking events. To find out more, go to www.hachettespeakersbureau.com or call (866) 376-6591.

Print book interior design by Sean Ford.

Library of Congress Cataloging-in-Publication Data

Names: Cohen, Sam, 1982- author.
Title: Sarahland : stories / Sam Cohen.
Description: First edition. | New York : Grand Central Publishing, 2021.
Identifiers: LCCN 2020030159 | ISBN 9781538735060 (hardcover) | ISBN 9781538735053 (ebook)
Classification: LCC PS3603.O378 A6 2021 | DDC 813/.6--dc23
LC record available at https://lccn.loc.gov/2020030159

ISBNs: 978-1-5387-3506-0 (hardcover), 978-1-5387-3505-3 (ebook)

Printed in the United States of America

LSC-C

Printing 1, 2021

For Sarahs, maybe-Sarahs, and Sarahs of the past and future.

CONTENTS

SARAHLAND

You've read the story, but there's no forest here, no wolf. No subterfuge is necessary; the boys are everywhere, out in the open, an infestation. Like cockroaches, they're most visible at night.

We stiletto them in the bellies and elbow them aside to clear a path down the hallway. We roll our eyes at their begging or pout and wag our fingers. We invite them in or pretend later we invited them in or slam the door in their faces or slam their fingers in the door. We grab one by the hand and continue down the hallway because he's cute or because we want to fend off other boys or because we want to make someone jealous. We pretend to be angry at them or we pretend to like them or we feel angry or we like them.

We have time to kill so we're watching a movie. The movie is *Heathers*. We're in sweats with the school's initials on our butts, and Sarah A. is eating broccoli that was once frozen but is now microwaved with yellow I Can't Believe It's Not Butter spray pooled in its florets. Last quarter, Sarah A. was bent on gaining the Freshman Fifteen, dousing her cafeteria fro-yo in chocolate syrup and gummi worms, ordering three a.m. pizza and saying, *eat girls*. College was supposed to be fun, and the Freshman Fifteen was proof you were having it. This quarter, though, Sarah A. was poking at the slight curve of her belly above her low-rise jeans and proclaiming, "I'm o-beast!" In this new phase, Sarah A.'s room smelled perpetually of microwaved broccoli and Febrezed-over farts.

It is a time when I have, without trying, fallen into a group of Sarahs—Sarah A., Sarah B., plus me. I am also a Sarah A., but no one calls me that. They call me Dr. Sarah, kind of mocking my premed major.

"Are you serious, you're so pretty," said the real Sarah A. when we first met in line at the frozen yogurt machine in the cafeteria. "You really don't need to do all that work." Sarah A. was always very certain about what you did or didn't need to do. But after she said it, I looked around in chem class and saw that, yeah, I was prettier than everyone.

"We're just here for our MRS degrees," Sarah B. spun around and added. Sarahs A. and B. were both five foot zero and bird-boned, with dark hair. Sarah A.'s was glossy and long and Sarah B.'s was poofy and pyramid-shaped. Next to them, I was a giant: four inches taller, salon-blond, an obvious nose job. "Ambition's attractive to guys, though," Sarah B. said. "You have to show them you're not like other girls or what-ever." She popped her lips, pocketed her gloss, and pulled the fro-yo lever. "I'm going to be prelaw until I get engaged. I'll go to law school if I have to, but hopefully I'll never have to *practice*."

It was a weird plan, so weird I wondered if Sarah B. was lying, like, was she stating her deepest fear as her goal so it would feel like success when it came true? My own secret plan was to be premed until I could figure out how to be one of those ocean scientists who spends a bunch of their time swimming naked in a pack of dolphins. It seemed like the beginning was the same—introductory bio, o-chem, et cetera and then somewhere a secret level unlocked, and you underwent a series of quests you didn't know about yet, and boom: dolphins.

We lived in a privately owned off-campus dormitory where 90 percent of the girls were named Sarah, or else Rachel, Alyssa, Jamie, Becca, Carrie, Elana, or Jen. The other 10 percent were named Bari, Shira, and Arielle. The whole dorm was Jewish. I never understood how these things happened. Nowhere on any of the dorm's advertising materials, which had succeeded in making me so excited to live with no parents in a building of studious eighteen-year-olds with a frozen yogurt machine, did it say the word *Jewish*, but it seemed wherever I went in my life, everyone was Jews. While I might think I was making independent choices and moving around freely in the world, it was as though a secret groove had been carved, and some invisible bumpers were going to push me gently back into that groove, the Jew groove, *Sarahland*, and Sarahland would trick me and trick me into thinking it was the entire world. It was confounding when I learned Jews were only 3 percent of the country, because, where was everybody else?

*   *   *

"We're like Heathers, but Sarahs," Sarah B. says.

"Sarahs are just Jewish Heathers," says Sarah A., touching up her manicure with a stroke of light pink.

"Sasha's totally the Winona Ryder," Sarah A. loud-whispers.

Sasha's phone rings a few minutes later and she springs out of bed and cups her hand over the mouth part as she sidles into the bathroom.

Sasha is Sarah A.'s roommate. She wears black leggings and tank tops and when we're there at ten p.m. flat-ironing and measuring shots of vodka into our cranberry juice or back in the room at three a.m. holding each other's hair back for puking and/or eating baked ziti pizza, Sasha is locked in the bathroom, on the phone with her boyfriend who goes to some other school in some other state. Her eyes are always puffy around the bottom, but she's skinny with naturally straight black hair and she doesn't seem to give a shit about us or what happens during our nights out and this makes her glamorous. I'm stuck in a horde of Sarahs but Sasha's on her own, crying alone in the bathroom or smoking alone on the dormitory's front stoop like someone's divorced mom.

"I want to be Winona Ryder," I say.

"You're so weird Dr. Sarah," says Sarah B.

"The Heathers are who is cool in this movie," says Sarah A. "Winona Ryder is demented. She's friends with the fat girl in the end."

It isn't the right way to even watch the movie I was pretty sure. You're supposed to want to be Winona Ryder, attached to a cool boy in a leather jacket who shoots up princesses and jocks and thereby shoots up *culture itself*. There seem to be only two options in *Heathers* and probably everywhere—

either you're attached to a group of girls and obsessed with diets and clothes or you're attached to a boy and obsessed with freedom and killing people. Sasha seems to be breaking the rule: she's attached to a boy, I guess, but he's an absent boy, a phone boy.

I am feeling unsure about my own level of pleasure, being subsumed into a Sarah horde but I'm also unsure how to extricate myself, where I would even go. My own roommate Shira clearly wants a bestie with whom to flat-iron while trying on clothes and taking vodka shots, but she's desperate and therefore a worse version of the thing I already have. The Sarahs at least have an ease with which they flat-iron and match shoes to outfits and take vodka shots and when something comes easily you can shrug it off like you barely even want it, and then you're more or less cool at least.

I ended up in this group partly because my best camp friend Ayelet was best friends with Sarah B. in high school. Every time I look at Sarah B. I remember how Ayelet and I swore to each other that camp was the only time/place that counted as Real Life, how we promised that our real selves would hibernate for ten months and only reemerge upon entry, next summer, into the North Woods. We held each other each August in the Minneapolis airport like a couple about to be separated by war, and wept.

Sarah B., I'm realizing as I watch her smash her eyelashes between those medieval-looking metal clampers, is only best friends with Ayelet's non-camp self, her impostor self, the shell of Ayelet. But now I'm stuck. Sarah B. invited me along on an early Bed Bath & Beyond trip based on our mutual Ayelet friendship and later invited me to sit with the Sarahs and soon

Sarah A. made a laminated chart of all our schedules so that we could only walk to and from class in a group and suddenly, without getting to fully decide, I was a Sarah.

The Nice Jewish Boys live in the dorm across the street, but for some reason, they are always in our dorm, leaning on hallway walls, sprawled across furniture, lying ghoulishly under our covers when we return from nights out. This is no grandma/wolf situation because there's no trickery—instead, the NJBs are in plain sight, drunk and wanting. They pound on our doors and shout our names, scrawl WHERE ARE YOU SARAHHHH on our dry-erase boards in all caps, materialize next to us while we're passed-out drunk. We wake, sometimes, with their slobber on our faces, their shoes in our sheets, their palms clawed around our boobs in a way they didn't try that hard to make look accidental.

Sarahs A. and B. are excellent at fighting the boy infestation. They spray disinfectant constantly, are always wiping things down. Possibly it's their pack mentality that keeps the boys away. They are clicked into each other, satisfied with doing nothing but taking cab rides to TCBY, working out on the elliptical downstairs, making popcorn and watching rom-coms until they meet their husbands, who certainly aren't going to be any of the infesting boys. The infesting boys aren't ready to be met yet, as husbands. I have a wandering eye though—I'm not looking for a husband but I am looking for something and, for the boys, my curiosity is like a small glob of peanut butter on the countertop in the summertime must be for ants. It makes them swarm.

* * *

Going Out is something we have to do every Thursday, Friday, and Saturday night. I'm not sure if any of us like it, but we show up for it like we show up for class, like we would show up for a job if we had one. I'm not sure how everyone found out about Going Out, how everyone discovered it will make these The Best Years of Our Lives but at eight p.m. on Thursdays, my roommate Shira starts automatically flat-ironing her hair and Sarah B. sends out a group text saying, *What are we doing tonight?* and Sarah A. says, *Meet in my room at 9.*

We walk down icy streets in high heels with peacoats covering our almost-bare skin and arrive at a bar where drinks are expensive and sit in a crowded judgey room and talk mostly to each other or else to people we like even less. In the best case scenario, Sarahs A. and B. feel that we might meet our husbands when we Go Out because the older boys are there, too, but this is a real outside chance so mostly we just go spend nine dollars apiece on cosmos and stand around in uncomfortable shoes.

We try on halter tops, tank tops, boatneck tops, cowl-neck tops, scoop-neck tops, cold-shoulder tops, tube tops, sparkly tops, sheer tops, stretchy tops, and silky tops. We use little paintbrushes to cover our zits and freckles. Every time we look at ourselves in the mirror, we jut our lips forward and gaze serious and sexy like we want to fuck our own reflections, and I wonder if any of us know what our actual faces even look like. We measure shots of vodka into cups of cranberry cocktail. We line up in a row and set our camera timers to take photos.

We lean over Sarah A.'s digital camera to scrutinize our looks. We can see ourselves a little differently in the camera's display screen than we do in the mirror. We're smiling now, convincing the viewfinder we're having the best time.

Sarah A. grabs the camera and pouts at it. "I hate my nose," she whines. "When I get my nose job, I'm totally taking photos of Dr. Sarah with me."

Sarah B. laughs, leaning over Sarah A.'s shoulder to look, too. "Good plan, I'm going to also. Dr. Sarah you truly have the best nose job in the whole dorm."

"Thanks," I say.

The truth was, I didn't even want my nose job. My parents had returned from Vegas "up fifty thousand" as they said. They pulled up in a limo, champagne-drunk and ecstatic, and announced their plan to divvy the money toward projects they'd been meaning to attend to: spider vein removal for my mother, a dining room table finally, a nose job for me. I cried and slammed my bedroom door and refused to go but somehow I ended up in the surgeon's chair shot up with drugs anyway and when I woke up my face was black and blue and three weeks later everyone agreed I looked like a shikse.

We put finishing touches on our looks and sing "Dancing Queen" while flat-ironing the bumps out of the backs of each other's hair.

"Come here, Dr. Sarah, you always have schmutz on your face," says Sarah A., clutching my jaw between her thumb and middle finger and turning my head from side to side for inspection. She licks a finger from her other hand and swats my cheek. We all check our little silver snap cases for our fake IDs and then we go to the bar.

*　　*　　*

The bar is called Stillwaters. Everyone calls it Stills but I think of it privately as the Stagnant Pond. The Pond's packed with Jewish girls from our dorm and Jewish boys from the boys' dorm plus all the kids who have ever lived in those dorms.

The boys are at the bar, but they barely talk to us there. At the bar, they're busy doing boy things—taking tequila shots and clapping each other on the back, shouting. We stand at the bar checking out other groups of girls and the truth is everyone looks like there was a memo: dewy skin and dark eyes, lightly glossed lips, hair meticulously flat-ironed, one of two models of jeans.

I chose this college because of a barista during my campus visit, I think. The barista's head was shaved on one side and she had piercings all the way up her ear. She seemed angry in general but like she liked me and I thought I would come to know girls like her here. But since Sarah A. created the Excel schedule chart, I only ever went anywhere in a pack. If it was blizzarding excessively, Sarah A. demanded we take a cab. The cab would go on streets we didn't normally take. I'd see a group of kids with Kool-Aid hair and fingerless gloves standing around outside a coffee shop smoking, probably talking about deep things. I felt like they might know the locations of some of the keys to the levels I'd need to pass through in order to be a dolphin scientist. But I was destined, it seemed, only to ever get glimpses outside the Jew groove from a cab window.

Tonight, it's blizzarding excessively. Luckily we have scarves with us, which we wrap around our heads and necks, *like bubushkas,* Sarah B. says, and run screaming in our stilettos through the wind and snow into the pizza place. Sarah A. gets a white spinach slice, I get a baked ziti slice, and Sarah B.

gets margherita, which she daubs with napkins until there's a pile of see-through napkins on the table and the cheese looks putty-dry.

Everyone who was at Stagnant Pond is in here now, drunk and eating various permutations of cheesy complex carbs. After pizza comes the worst part, which is the part where we have to stand out on the street corner in our stilettos with two hundred other people, all of whom were in the Stagnant Pond with us, and then the pizza place. Here is where we start to talk to other people for the first time. An older boy named Jon approaches and says, "Hey, how you been?" and I say "good" and he says "Cool wanna come over?" The thing is I'd gone home with him the week before and I was starting to understand that this is how it went: you gave someone a blow job and then once you gave the blow job and they never called, you felt rejected and a little sad even if you hadn't liked them very much and so then you stood outside the next week with wind whipping snowflakes in your face in case they wanted another one. I'm not looking forward to trying to make my way through the boy infestation in my dorm and also I'm freezing and don't want to stand in the snow anymore, so I say okay, and we run two blocks to his apartment, where I get under his covers, give him a blow job, and fall asleep.

When I wake up, I hear a voice say to me, *To thine own self be true!* I collect phrases I like, like this, in my quote book and eventually they become internal voices, reverberating in my head as though they're my conscience or spirit guides. I feel guilty about giving a blow job I knew in advance I'd find unpleasant, to a boy I knew would never call, and then I feel, I am a social animal! We're hardwired to form complex societies, so why should I be some loner animal that is trying to resist everything asked of me? I can stand around in the freezing wind and then give boys blow jobs if that is the ritual of my society! I put on my tank top and jeans from the night before and walk out of the older boy's apartment in my stilettos, headache searing behind my eyes, in the snow.

I thought college would be exactly like summer camp, that there was a magic formula where you put a bunch of girls in an enclosed space without parents and we'd become Real. But, I deduced after major sleuthing, two factors were getting in the way: money and boys.

Neither existed at camp and here both were everywhere. The annual social we'd have with the nearby boys' camp was the worst day of the year: everyone unearthed makeup and flat-irons stowed under bunk beds for the other fifty-eight days of camp. Normally we spent our days and nights sailing and tie-dyeing towels and weaving macramé wall hangings and trying to get up on one water ski and singing along to Joni Mitchell and the Indigo Girls around a literal bonfire but suddenly on the day of the social we only cared about having the straightest hair and the clearest skin and someone was always being a cunt to her best friend and someone was always crying.

Here we had the boy infestation, and money that came in seemingly endless forms. One form was the purses that hung on everyones' doors, Pradas and Kate Spades and Louis Vuittons. I didn't understand these purses, what they meant, but I sort of understood they had something to do with the Holocaust. These girls' grandmas wanted them to know that here in America they could not be turned to soap, and these bags proved it. The bags were a display of patriotism; American flags might be goyishe and tacky but Prada bags were little markers of belief in liberty and the pursuit of happiness in the land of the free. Granddaughters could send pictures of themselves standing in a row of flat-ironed and haltered girls, each with a Prada bag, and their bubbes would feel, *these girls were so safe.*

I don't have a Prada bag. My own mother celebrates her freedom by finding excellent deals at Loehmann's on purses she swears look expensive but, I can see now, do not. My Loehmann's purses are one of the reasons the other Sarahs feel like they need to teach me how to live.

"Dr. Sarah," Sarah A. says. We're sitting at a lunch table eating salads. It's the day after the blow job. "I've been paying close attention. You actually eat super healthy foods, so I think you're just eating too much of them."

Embarrassment blooms rosacea-like all over my skin. Eating is the world's greatest shame. I just learned the word *slut-shaming* from a flyer posted to one of the student union bulletin boards, but as far as I can tell, you can swallow dick in any quantity and no one cares. It's true that if you were bad at fighting the boy infestation you were known as a slut, which I was. People thought being a slut made it ridiculous that I also planned to be a doctor, but I was a science major and I didn't see how the two were correlative. Anyway, food and not sex was the real source of humiliation.

"Maybe try just eating half of whatever you were going to eat," says Sarah A.

Sarah A. is putting me in an impossible position. Either I'm going to eat half and act like I didn't know how to go on a diet by myself or I'm going to keep eating the same amount and make Sarah A. think I have no self-control.

I'm fatter than the other Sarahs, but I haven't always been fat. Fourteen transformed my thighs into Spanish hams that spread out wide and flat, sticking to bleachers and peeling off painfully in summertime. My chest sprung overnight C cups. At fifteen, I reduced my calorie count to 400 daily. Four hundred seemed like enough for basic metabolic processes, yet few enough to strip the meat from my thighs and breasts, to make me less like a bucket of chicken and more like a super skinny girl. On 400 calories, I could wear crop halters and black leggings to musical practice. On 400 calories, my mom rewarded me with shopping trips. On 400 calories, I no longer went poo, which was nice because poo had always disgusted me and I no longer bled from my vag, which was also nice because I had been praying not to bleed from my vag ever since I read *Are You There God? It's Me, Margaret* and really really didn't identify with Margaret but did learn about certain kinds of negotiations you could make with God. Four hundred calories made it difficult to hang out with other people, but this, too, was okay, since only camp was Real Life. I could go home and sit in my room and record tape-letters to Ayelet and listen to tape-letters from her, especially the mix tapes she'd make at the end when she was done talking, Tori and Ani, Fiona and Liz. I listened to her tapes like they were church, or what I imagined church would be like. I listened for secret meanings, for lines about me. At open campus lunch, I could drive home in order to eat one microwaved frozen veggie patty. After musical practice, I declined fro-yo invitations from the naturally skinny girls for whom sugar-free was promise enough. When the taffeta dress I was meant to wear as my costume for the musical arrived, the entire top half fell off my shoulders and down to my waist where it gathered in ripples around my hips. "Did you send in the wrong measurements or did you shrink?" the woman fitting me joked. "You girls are so tiny," she said. She went to find an extra, smaller dress somewhere, and I beamed.

At camp, we bonded by sneaking chocolate into our cabins. In the dorm, though, chocolate's allowed so we have to sneak vodka. One tiny shot glass is 100 calories and then you have to chase it with some kind of juice, and at three a.m. you're starving and when you get to the pizza place, spinning with vodka and a snow-blasted face, it's impossible not to devour the whole slice.

It's Sarah A. who has, in the first place, encouraged us to get burritos, beer and vegan hot wings, Doritos and wine. Sarah A. with her long black hair and super selective smile and overall tininess is convincing. And while the other girls are still petite *even with* their fifteen pounds, I am fat now and trying to distract from it with glitter powder on my eyes and décolletage. While the other girls stay in their packs, puking and having snacks, I am bent on being independent. I relish the time after two a.m. when there's no laminated information about where I should be and I'm suddenly free. But I'm also drunk, even after puking and/or snacks, and terrible at fending off my own boy-infestation—I wake with them lying on top of me, breathing into my mouth.

This is what eating leads to. You start recklessly putting things into your body and you just become permeable. When

I become a dolphin, I will eat only raw fish, catching them in my teeth as they swim by.

Even though all the kids in the private dorm have a list of the easiest classes the university offers and enroll en masse for Scandinavian Literature in order to meet their Comm B requirement, I care about learning and do not care about Scandinavia. I am a rebel in this small way. So spring quarter I enroll in a class called Integrated Liberal Studies, which promises to "imagine a method of critical thought that produces writing with the potential to change the world." This is exciting—I've been discovering the pleasure of getting stoned and writing in my journal under the covers—and secretly I guess I do want to change the world, to make it void of money and boys at least.

For the first day of Integrated Liberal Studies, I wear my edgiest outfit, a kelly-green minidress over jeans, and let my hair dry wavy instead of flat-ironing it. Still, I feel like an impostor, an obvious JAP, when I see the other looks in the lecture hall—dreadlocks and pants held together by patches; cropped hair dyed yellow. Leaving class, I see Sasha, in a gray V-neck and skinny jeans, putting a notebook into her brown leather bag, which looks like the kind the professors have. Sasha's hair falls to mid-back, straight without being flat-ironed, just a few choppy layers in the front. She looks like a celebrity photographed at Starbucks in the "Stars—They're Just Like Us!" section but also like a serious philosophy student.

"Hey," she says. "How's it going?"

I have never been someone who knew how to answer this question. I nod enthusiastically.

15

"I'm surprised to see you here," she says. "I didn't know you cared about philosophy. No offense."

"I don't know," I reply.

"Wanna get lunch?" Sasha asks. I do. I text the Sarahs: *Have to meet with my TA; I'll see you guys later*, but I worry that they'll wait at our meeting spot anyway, so I lead Sasha down a side street where we'll miss them. We walk to the Mediterranean place where you get a plate of whatever combination of vegetarian things they're serving that day for $5: spinach pie, olives, hummus, rice, cucumbers. We start arguing about the thinkers from class. I love Jean-Jacques Rousseau, who wants us to live free of society, to throw off our JAP-y chains and roam wild like bears or geese.

Sasha rolls her eyes, pours hot sauce into her soup. "Rousseau is just some clueless dude with a dumb romantic fantasy of living like the savage brown people," she says, using bouncy single-digit air quotes around *savage brown people*. I'd never heard anyone talk like this, in a way that could make me feel like the Great Men were just dudes we could know. It makes so much sense though. What other kinds of dudes would they be? "It's all about Rawls," she insists. "The original position. We have to design our morality imagining we're all sitting in a boardroom, all starting over, and we don't know where in society we'll start out."

Rawls is boring to me. I hate boardrooms. I don't need society, I tell her—I can roll around in the dirt and eat fruit from trees.

Sasha rolls her eyes. "You're such a white girl," she says.

Sasha was raised in a Jewish suburb, but she was born in the Caribbean. This is part of what makes her a little exciting, I know: you look at the Jewish girls and just see your own issues, your same mom trauma, a little fun-house-mirrored but still. The white kind of goyim are mysterious, too, but not in a way we care about—we mock their taste for mayonnaise and floral print, for promptness and guns. We avoid them in our classes without even trying.

"Let's get a drink," Sasha says once we've eaten every single thing on our plates. It seems like Sasha can eat whatever she wants, like eating involves neither shame nor calculations, and she still ends up a super skinny girl. We go into a bar with our fake IDs, where Sasha orders a dark-colored microbrew. The bar is dim and empty, we sit on stools. I somehow hadn't realized you could just wander into a bar in the daytime. The possibilities for interacting with the world feel expanded and I don't know what to order. I've never been in a bar except for Going Out on Thursday through Saturday nights, and it seems like it would be weird to order a Cosmo here. I ask for what Sasha has. It feels cool to drink something heavy and bitter on purpose.

I tell Sasha about the boy I've now given two blow jobs to, only I don't phrase it like that, I say, *hooked up with*, and how I can barely find anything special about him to like, except that now that he's not calling me I feel like *I'm* not special and want his attention. And I start thinking, well, he does have a really cute smile and he plays the guitar, which is cool, and he talks so little that he's probably secretly really smart.

"I'm going to read you bell hooks," Sasha says, and fishes a book from her professor bag, opens it. She reads an underlined sentence: "If any female feels she needs anything beyond herself to legitimate and validate her existence, she is already giving away her power to be self-defining."

"I guess," I say. I only feel real, I know, as a reflection, as part of a Sarah horde. I feel like Sasha's full of shit also because what is she crying about in the bathroom, then, if she doesn't want to be legitimated.

"I want to at least not have to be legitimated by anyone in our stupid dorm," Sasha clarifies, as if reading my mind. "Or by boys, generally."

I feel a surge of very intense feeling in my chest because I've never heard anyone acknowledge that our dorm is stupid or that boys ruin everything.

"You think our dorm is stupid?" I say. "I do, too."

"It's a Jewish marriage machine," Sasha shrugs. Sasha has this cheery nihilistic vibe that makes it seem impossible that she spends her evenings crying in the bathroom.

"I think boys are stupid, too," I blurt.

"Yeah. I made out with my girl TA last weekend," Sasha says.

I don't know what to say to that; I feel shocked in a way like the world has exploded open and anything on earth is possible, like I could be a dolphin after all.

"What about your boyfriend?" I ask.

"I think I'm done with him," Sasha says. "I'm over Jewish boys."

She says it as though I haven't heard her crying in the bathroom over and over, as though she's the coolest person on earth.

"It's not like they'll ever be serious about me anyway," she adds. "I'm, like, a fun island vacation before they find their Jewish wives." What she's describing sounds painful, but she is smiling, so I don't know what to say.

A pasty bearded dude in a beanie and flannel next to us asks Sasha what she's reading.

"It's bell hooks," says Sasha, "but we'd like to be left alone to enjoy each other's company please."

The guy looks startled, and when Sasha turns back to me, he mutters "Bitch" under his breath but loud enough that we can hear. I look at the way Sasha's hair curves around her elbow, the way a combination of smoking and crying has made her look so sick-good in her V-neck tee tucked into high-waisted jeans.

We walk back to the dorm sharing a clove cigarette and talking about bands Sasha likes. She promises to burn me CDs. It's my first clove and it makes me feel like we're art kids in some movie in the '70s instead of 2000s JAPs, like with Sasha I can time travel. When we get back inside, boys are seeping from wall crevices and popping around corners. Sasha waves her Longchamp tote around like a dangerous wand and the boys seep back into the walls.

The following Thursday night, Sarah B. IMs us: *Hey girls, what's the plan?*

Sarah A. IMs back, *My room at 9? Everyone's going to Stills.*

Sarah B. sends back a sideways smiley. *Fun! See you girls soon!*

I feel a sick fluttering feeling. I feel weird about being in Sarah and Sasha's room in my halter and glitter décolletage, weird about Sasha watching me take vodka shots with the Sarahs, or else only seeing her as she slams the bathroom door behind her, revealing her over-it-ness to be a lie. I need to do what I can to preserve our idea of ourselves as girls who day drink, arguing about philosophy. I write back, *I'm feeling kind of sick, I think I'm gonna stay in.*

Are you really sick, Dr. Sarah, or are you just being weird?

The Sarahs are always calling me weird and it's oddly effective. I don't want to be weird. I hesitate. *I'm going to stay in*, I type.

She's being weird, Sarah B. IMs. I roll my eyes and shut my computer.

I sit on my bed with the Bible open in front of me. We're reading it for the Integrated Liberal Studies class, focusing on the red parts, what Jesus said. It's my first introduction to Jesus. Jesus is all right. I always thought Jesus was tacky because I've mostly seen him rendered in pastels made out of cheap-looking plastic or all boo-hoo anorexic and tacked up for display. Along with reading, I'm sitting on my purple flannel sheet watching Shira straighten her hair in her vanity mirror with adjustable zoom and lighting. "Do I look okay?" she asks, watching me watch her in the reflection. Shira is slightly too fat to ask if she looks fat; it's embarrassing, I think, for the word *fat* to even come out of her mouth. The best she could try to make you say was *okay*.

"Yeah," I say, not really wanting to say anything more, even though I think she would look actually pretty if she didn't look so anxious and sad. She has the right brand of jeans and the right pointy-toed boots, a good haircut and highlights, heavily mascaraed yellow-green eyes. Somehow I can't be nice to Shira, though. She wants so badly this thing that I feel stuck in. The dorm's Shiras didn't cluster the way we did and even though Shira has friends of camp friends in here, too, none of them seem to want to hang out with her. "Where are you going?" I ask, deadpan and staring like she's probably going somewhere dumb.

20

"I think people are going to Stills?" she says like a question. "Jenny's coming to get me."

Jenny is Shira's one friend and it's clear they don't like each other that much, just both failed to work their ways into the group of girls they'd wanted. It's sad to see them together— Jenny has curls cut into a bushy shape, a too-obvious nose job, and darting owl eyes that make her look like she wants to gouge yours out. She arrives, and after she and Shira greet each other awkwardly, they leave. I lie on my bed and read about Jesus.

Like an hour later there's a knock on my door. I don't want to deal with any of the infesting boys. *SARAHHH* one yells. I don't respond. He keeps banging. I realize that the boys aren't slithering through the crack in the bottom of the door or emerging from the walls: Shira's just opening the door and letting them in. She's so desperate to be a cool girl, I think, and the way to be a cool girl is to be in cahoots with the boys. I feel mad at Shira and then smile a little at the loyalty of the boys, who wait just for me.

The knocking stops finally and then starts again and persists and I hear a decisive voice say, "Sarah!" but the voice is female. It's Sasha's voice. I'm wearing sweats with the school's initials on the butt and even though she's seen me in these sweats countless times in her room, I feel embarrassed by them now. "One sec," I call. I throw on a floral baby-doll dress that covers my butt. Is a baby-doll dress with sweats cool and arty looking? I'm not sure but I look in the mirror and the overall impression is: cute. I gather my unstraightened hair into two giant buns, with fuzzy waves dangling from each. I open the door.

"Hey," I say.

"Hey," says Sasha. "I was wondering if you felt okay."

"Yeah," I say. "I just didn't feel like Going Out."

"Cool, I figured," she says, walking past the threshold and into my room, just like the boys do. "Wanna listen to music?"

She's brought Jameson. I've never tried whiskey and I feel, like, how did she come across these things in this vodka cranberry dorm? It tastes like men, I think, or it tastes like we're men. We sit side by side on my bed and she opens her laptop and plays songs from Napster. Portishead, Zero 7, Radiohead, Erykah Badu. The Sarahs like Billy Joel and REO Speedwagon and with whiskey and Portishead swimming through my head I feel new.

"What do you want to be?" I ask her. It seems like this should be the obvious question of college because ostensibly we're all here to become something but people mostly don't talk about it, acting instead like we're just going to be here in college forever.

"Civil rights lawyer," she says. "What about you?"

"Ocean scientist," I say, "but only secretly. Publicly, I'm premed."

Sasha laughs. "But probably you'll be a middle school biology teacher and marry a doctor, right?" She swigs whiskey and then passes me the bottle.

"What?" I say.

"I mean ultimately you're a Sarah," says Sasha.

I feel stung. I felt like we were connecting, like she was seeing me in a way that was different from how the Sarahs see me, like with Sasha I was becoming not *a* Sarah but just Sarah, the only Sarah, Sasha and Sarah. I say, "I'm not." I sip from the whiskey bottle.

We're silent after that, sitting against the wall and smoking weed and listening to a whole Radiohead album and sometimes commenting on it. *There are two colors in my head,* it says, and says it again. The voice sounds too fast, all over the place, like it can't get a grip on something important. It's kind of how I feel, stoned and sitting on my bed with Sasha, who feels I'm ultimately a Sarah. She can't see the other color, I think.

The next day the Sarahs IM to meet in the lobby at eleven. We get breakfast like we always do on Fridays and then we go to the town's expensive jeans store. Sarahs A. and B. somehow know how to talk to the perfect-looking girls who work in this store that has clearly hired a multiethnic staff of girls who each look like the Barbie version of their ethnic group.

"What washes do you have in the new Citizens of Humanity?" Sarah A. asks. "I'm looking for something with a medium wash but I'm short-waisted," explains Sarah B. I stand there feeling weird as the other Sarahs chat with the girls who work there using terminology I seem to have failed to learn. "Look at this white V-neck, Sar," Sarah B. says to Sarah A., ignoring me. I look at the V-neck, too, even though I haven't been invited to. "It's sixty-eight dollars for a T-shirt?" I whisper loudly. Both Sarahs glare. "Here, Dr. Sarah," Sarah A. says, passing me a purple halter. "This would be cute on you for Going Out."

"I don't know," I say. The truth is the store is so expensive that it feels pointless to look at anything.

"Come on," she says.

"It's cute, Dr. Sarah," says Sarah B. "You need to show your boobs more."

I try it on. Both Sarahs and two of the salesgirls gush and gush and gush and I can't see what's so special about the purple halter, but it begins to feel as though I'm stupid for not being able to see what's so special about the purple halter, and without the ability to discern whether it is or is not special, I have no language with which to defend my disinclination to buy it.

When the salesgirl swipes my debit card for $61.48 including tax, I feel like she's stealing my money.

Still, I wear the halter to Sarah A. and Sasha's room that night for Going Out and Sasha says "That top looks amazing on you" and I blush. Sasha keeps looking at me and while she's looking she says, "I want to go out with you guys."

"Sashy!" Sarah A. says. "Yes, come." She doesn't say it fakely but in a genuine way because they're friends, too, Sarah A. and Sasha, even if Sarah A. makes fun of Sasha and thinks she's totally weird.

Sasha puts on a yellow T-shirt from Urban Outfitters that says Blondes Have More Fun, which is funny, I think, and then flat-irons her already straight black hair and does her lip gloss and eyeliner.

"Where are we going?" Sarah B. asks and Sarah A. says "Stills?"

Sasha says, "I hate Stills." It's so brave I think, to say that.

"I kind of hate Stills, too," I try.

Sarah A. stops mid brushstroke, hip cocked, one side of her hair stretched all the way out in a diagonal. She meets my eyes in the mirror. "Fine," says Sarah A. She's not the type to fight when her authority's not respected, which is part of why, I realize, I like her. If you don't know what you want, she'll definitely tell you, but if you do, she'll roll her eyes and then lay off.

"Let's do something more chill," Sasha says.

Chill, I realize, means boots instead of stilettos. I stop in my room and change into tall brown boots, a knee-length denim skirt. I can't find tights so I wear thermals underneath, thick wool socks with snowflakes on them. I keep the purple halter on and it's a good outfit, I think. I put on my labradorite necklace to signify to the chill people of wherever we go that even if I don't look like it, I have a connection to the universe, that I am available for a conversation that might be called "deep." I throw a puffy on over the whole ensemble and we meet in the lobby.

It's almost 40 degrees so we're comfortable walking downtown in our scarves and hats. We check out the people standing in lines, look at what brand their parkas are and how they stand and how their laughs sound. We peer into doorways. Sarah B. gets intrigued by a blue-lit martini bar full of adults.

"Come on," Sasha says, "I know a place." We follow her down a set of stairs into a bar in a basement with a dirty checkerboard floor and a pool table.

"We are *definitely* not going to meet our husbands here," Sarah B. says, brows hoisted, and Sasha and I exchange a look that feels so intimate, we both break out laughing.

"We're just here to chill," Sasha says.

"I don't know how to chill!" Sarah A. confesses. Her eyes bug out and then she cracks up. This is why I like her, too, her solidity, the way she never tries to pretend to be someone she's not.

We get drinks and then Sasha wants to play pool. Of course Sasha knows how to play pool, which of course is also shocking since she spends most nights crying in the bathroom. Sasha has a secret day life, I realize. Sarah A. weirdly knows how to play, too, and coaches Sarah B. while Sasha coaches me, standing behind me and talking about angles and ricochet. I do all right and Sasha is like, "fuck yes," low-fiving me and clinking beers and I feel amazing.

Two guys come up, hippies, in my mind, because they're wearing cargo pants and T-shirts, because they have scruffy beards and one has a necklace made out of some kind of fibrous material, with beads.

"You girls are skilled," one says.

"Yeah we are," says Sasha.

The other Sarahs stay huddled at the corner of the table as though these blond boys are strange animals.

The guys introduce themselves and immediately I realize I haven't retained their names—Sean or Steve or Seth and Mike or Matt or Jeff.

We introduce ourselves and then I glance at Sarahs A. and B. at the other corner of the table. They're engaged in conversation, like, they're not going to bother.

Sean or Steve asks where we live and we tell him.

"Whoa, you girls seem too cool for that dorm," he says. "You don't seem snobby or stuck up at all."

"Thanks," I say.

"You girls want to dance?" asks Seth or Greg.

"Sure," says Sasha and she tilts her head back and downs the rest of her beer. The boys are practically drooling because it's all boys want, someone skinny with heavy hair that curls around her elbows but who doesn't act like whatever they think of as a girl.

We all go over to the dance floor and the Sarahs kind of follow but stay huddled and apart. They're wearing 7 for All Mankind jeans and Michael Stars T-shirts but they might as well be wearing pastel coats and pillbox hats and have their hands shoved in muffs. Bon Jovi is playing and we're singing and pumping our hands in the air and I think, *We'd never be doing this at the Stagnant Pond.* The boys come back with shots and we swallow them.

Then "River of Dreams" comes on and the Sarahs can't help themselves. They slide their Prada baguettes up beneath their armpits and jump around and sing. They stay and sing through "Sweet Caroline" and "Don't Stop Believin'."

Sasha stands and watches, laughing and shaking her head. "This music is so terrible," she says.

Sarah A. motions for us all to huddle and we do.

"This was fun but I think we should go," Sarah A. says.

"I'm gonna hang for a little bit," says Sasha.

"I'll stay, too," I say.

"With these anti-Semites?" Sarah B. demands.

"They're not anti-Semites," I sigh.

"Oh really? Did you hear what they said about our dorm being snobbish?"

"Our dorm *is* snobbish."

"Okay, but you know that he means something different than you when he says that, right?"

I roll my eyes. "I'm not going to marry them," I say, "I just want to jump around and sing and stuff."

"Fine," Sarah A. shrugs. "Be careful and stay with Sashy though, okay?"

"I will," I say.

"Promise?" Sarah B. asks. "Don't get drunk."

Both Sarahs kiss my cheek and leave the basement and the boys go get shots and come back and we take them. This happens a few times. We get drunk.

Sasha and I dance to Outkast's "Hey Ya," which kind of moves us away from the boys, because we're moving our arms like robots and just vibrating our bodies all crazy like they're being controlled by a remote somewhere outside of us. We're crashing our bodies into each other only it's not us doing it, it's the music making us crash and vibrate and run each other all the way into the wall and laugh hysterically and then this horrible thing happens: Sasha looks up and locks eyes with this other girl right behind me and her jaw drops and she leaps past me and I spin around and they're embracing. The girl has a little golden fro, a septum ring and black overalls, and she is so so pretty. *How does Sasha know this girl? Her secret day life?* No one in the dorm has a septum ring. And then I realize they're still embracing, embracing longer than I'd ever embrace either other Sarah, and kind of rocking, and I realize she's the girl TA Sasha made out with, she must be. She looks sophisticated, like she knows things. Sasha introduces me, *This is Shay!*, but their arms stay wrapped around each other, right around each other's hips and Shay is rubbing the bare skin of Sasha's shoulder blade with her hand, with its opal and tourmaline rings and lavender nails.

For some reason my face heats up and my eyes start burning. "I have to go to the bathroom," I say. I lock myself in a stall and sit on the toilet. I ball my hands into fists and push my fists against the wall, and then kind of let my body fall to the side, gravity helping the side of my face, my shoulder and arm, connect with the plastery wall. I fall again and again, each time a little harder than the last, the time between falls lessening. I don't know why, everything just feels really intense and it feels like I have to meet that intensity with something equal. When I've collided with the wall enough times, I stay sitting on the toilet and sort of gulp air.

I look in the mirror and see my face is flecked with red on one side, I've coaxed the blood out, made it rise, in dots, to the surface. Oh well, I think. It's dark out there, and everyone's drunk. The skin isn't broken. I wipe away the black smear under my right eye and head back out.

Sasha and Shay are standing at the bar, Shay's arm around Sasha's waist and her fingers tucked into one of Sasha's belt loops. They call me over and say they got us shots. It's Jägermeister, all licorice and gross.

Sean or Seth or Jeff appears out of nowhere and grabs my hand, says "Let's dance." I'm obviously a third wheel and so I go with him to the dance floor and we're dancing, kind of grinding. Sasha and Shay appear next to us, staring into each other's eyes and doing robot dance type stuff and laughing. I feel my face starting to burn again.

"Hey, I'm gonna head out," I shout to everyone.

"Sarah, stay," Sasha says.

"I'm tired," I say. "It was nice to meet you," I tell Shay.

"It was nice to meet you," says Shay sounding legitimately full of joy, which makes sense because she's some sort of poli sci genius who is getting to study as like a job and is also making out with Sasha.

"You gonna be okay walking back?" Sasha yells.

"It's like two point five blocks away."

"Okay, yeah."

"I'll walk her," says Seth-Sean.

"No need," I say.

"Come on," he says. He grabs my hand and we walk past the dance floor, up the stairs, and out to the street.

"So your friend's, like, a lesbian?" Seth-Sean asks.

"I'm not really sure," I say. "I think she's just experimenting, as they say."

"That's cool. You really are a very cool girl," Seth-Sean says. "It's surprising that you live in that weird dorm."

"Thanks," I say. I feel like he's just now picking up on my labradorite necklace and believing in it, believing that I'm connected to the universe.

"Do you want to come home with me?" he asks.

It feels sudden. I look at him and realize that maybe I am not that chill, not chill enough to go home with non-Jewish boys, or maybe it's just that after seeing Sasha and Shay together, the idea of this big mannish person touching me feels gross.

"No," I say. "I'm tired. I just want to go home."

"Okay," he says. "That's totally cool."

"Thanks," I say, and then wonder what I'm thanking him for. "So what do you study?"

"Environmental science," he says. "It's great. I'm going to Costa Rica next year to study the cloud forests."

"That's so amazing. I didn't even know environmental science existed. I'd love to do something like that. Cloud forests!"

He laughs. "It exists. Yeah, it's pretty cool. Are you sure you don't want to go home with me? I can show you some really amazing nature videos."

"Yeah, I'm sure," I say. I smile. "Nice try, though."

We get to the doors of my dorm.

"Can I come in?" he asks.

"No, no," I say. "I really am tired. Just take my number." This feels like an effective way to fight off an infesting boy that I am well practiced in—give him hope.

"It's okay, I'll just find you Out somewhere," he says. "Good night." He hugs me and I hug him back. I let it be a long hug, let him pull me in close and bury his face in my neck and let his hands slide down to my waist but then they slide down to my butt and from the butt, he lifts me, pushes me into the entrance vestibule of the dorm and against the wall. I'm not practiced in saying no so instead I say "What are you doing?" and "Hey put me down" or maybe I don't say that and what's coming out is a confused unghhh sound and then my skirt's scrunched up around my hips and my thermals are down, so easily, like he's done it all, lifted me and unzipped and slipped right in, in a single move and I try wresting free but I can't and all I can think is someone might walk in. It smells like a clashing blend of expensive perfumes that in their combination have lost all subtlety and become something nauseating and then it's over. He drops me, and says "I'm really sorry."

"It's okay," I say.

And it is, I think, okay. It's like everything.

I reenter Sarahland.

In my room, there's an infesting boy lying in my bed, looking dumb with the bill of his baseball cap curved like a duck or whatever and eyes closed and mouth open, periodically snorting up at the ceiling. His dumbness seems kind of sweet, I think. I change into pajamas my mom sent in a care package, pink flannel covered in cartoon lipsticks, and get in bed. I turn the boy on his side and push him toward the wall. He whines "Sarahhhh" but I just say "ssh" and then he resumes snorting and I crawl in, avoid touching him as much as possible, and try to sleep.

NAKED FURNITURE

Sarah dressed for the appointment in a blue polka-dot dress with stiff puff sleeves and a pointed collar. She curled her bangs with a hot round brush, thickened her lashes, and painted her lips with the new product she'd gotten, dipping the little brush into the gooey red. It took her nearly a quarter of an hour to create a convincing lip shape, even when she tried to stay within the carbon-made lines of her own. The line between lip skin and plain skin, she discovered painting, is less clear than you think. Sarah put on white socks and lace-up leather oxfords. When she looked at her reflection in the mirror she saw someone who wasn't herself. Who she saw was a Girl In A Story.

This was good. Sarah wanted to be in a story. Sarah's life used to be a story. She was—recently, even!—baby-eyed and fruitlike, adorable and marriageable and getting all A's at the state university. She had been envied for her clear setup for success in the story that was The Only Story but had been too innocent and envy-free to notice any of the envy. She blithely accepted dates or turned them down, accepted scholarship checks for achievement, an invitation to study abroad.

But Sarah returned from abroad itchy, her hair chopped and bleached. She had seen that life could be an endless parade of tiny coffees and cigarettes, that people didn't have to walk around with shitty plastered cheer that only advertised the shame they felt at their own dissatisfaction at living in a life-destroying system. In her junior year at the state university, Sarah switched her major to English and in her new English classes, Sarah had new strong feelings she wasn't afraid to share. In response to Sarah's bleach and her feelings, Sarah's classmates offered to lend her books, and these books, the ones that wound up in Sarah's backpack and then her bed, scandalized her. Or maybe Sarah was already scandalized by everything she was learning at school—she was scandalized by the girls around her with their Fendi sunglasses and single-serve microwave popcorn and the gazillions of invisible workers she learned about in a documentary in Sociology who worked like entirely in these girls' service. She was scandalized by the boys who lowered their voices to sound dumb and tough, who talked to her like she was made of synthetic materials but whom she made out with anyway. She was scandalized by the trash cans full of plastic and the invisible dying polar bears. But the books from Sarah's classmates made Sarah feel like there might be other ways to respond to scandal. Or at least like she wasn't alone in feeling sick and weird. The books worked on Sarah like paint stripper. There had been a store in Sarah's hometown called the Naked Furniture Store and this is how Sarah felt, like naked furniture, like something embarrassingly unfinished, something that could be anything. Sarah as Naked

Furniture let herself be remade by the books: she realized she had always been looking for a way out of the story that was The Only Story. It could have been anything, but the books showed up. She started to identify with that beehived chick on that black-and-white poster in used bookstores: "She is too fond of books and it has turned her brain." The brain-turning pushed Sarah to make odder choices regarding the outside of her head, too—a green streak, a razored scalp, a septum piercing—which in turn yielded stranger books in her backpack, weirder movies privately screened on classmates' foamy mattresses. In the movies Sarah was watching, story had been deconstructed or was hard to follow, everything was just a bunch of disconnected moments. Music no longer had choruses or anything catchy.

Sarah gazed at the story-girl in the mirror and immediately thought of that bananafish story from high school, the one about the ways materialism makes women selfish and therefore incapable of caring for their tortured bb boyfriends. This wasn't going to be that story—this was going to be a different story. Anyway, Sarah had no tortured bb boyfriend because she was, at the moment, riding the second wave and starting to believe in lesbianism as a moral imperative, and so it was fine if she was into herself and also materials.

Way before Sarah read all the paint-stripping books, she read a book where someone wrote that it was like America had been tilted and everything that wasn't tightly screwed down had slid to Los Angeles. Sarah's old friends at her state university were deeply weirded out by Sarah's sudden transformation and new English friends. They whispered about Sarah and gave her weird looks and some of them told her it seemed like she "needed help." Sarah felt partly reborn via the books and her English friends, but she also felt like she couldn't be *fully* reborn in the Fendi-shaded gaze of the girls she used to be friends with. These friends' responses to Sarah's partial rebirth unscrewed Sarah. Loose, Sarah slid down an invisible chute all the way to a studio apartment in a building in Hollywood with seven feral cats living on the doorstep and small piles of human shit thronging the side entrance. Scientologists in their polos stood on the surrounding corners looking vacant and cloned.

Sarah valued this small space that was hers only, a space in which she was free of the Fendi-shaded gazes and the plastic trashers and her mom. To pay its rent, Sarah was helping small children with reading as part of a program funded by the city. This was the kind of job you could get if you'd ended up deciding to be an English major in college, one that didn't pay enough to live, one that didn't put you in touch with anyone with whom you might want to get a drink, even if you could afford one. Sarah could do two tutoring sessions back-to-back before she was exhausted: she hated the moms for their sad hopeful gazes or else for their indifference. She hated the way faces of five-year-olds sounding out c-a-t for the first time would light up, ignorant of their future as semi-literate and catless workers in service of the worker-exploiting and earth-destroying Grand Shitpile. She hated this program that sent untrained white girls into people's homes as though everyone's real issue is not having a white mommy to read about cats with. Sarah hated biking in the heat; the way her thighs sweat and stuck together made her feel fat. Plus men made so many loud gross kissy noises and shouted so many hey mamas at her that she'd taken to biking with one middle finger extended. It was so much work.

Sarah hated tutoring but also wasn't sure what to do with all her time that wasn't tutoring. She read a little and laid on her bed a lot. It's really easy, in a studio apartment, to end up lying on your bed a lot. No one told Sarah that if you're going to just abandon the story that is The Only Story, you have to *replace* it with something—you have to, like, fight for social justice or become a genius artist. Sarah felt loosely inclined toward art and social justice but she wasn't really doing anything about those loose inclinations.

Soon, Sarah was in a place in her life where she couldn't wake up to move her car for street cleaning. She accrued parking tickets, which were swept into the trash or sticky and matted into corners of her studio apartment where they grew soft hairs or laminated themselves into the floor, still faintly legible. Soon, Sarah was in a place in her life where she threw out plates. Her plates were like sedimentary rocks—hardened layers of former food, blue-speckled with mold, would just merge with and then *become the plates* at some point, the point at which it was time to deposit them in the trash.

It was a garment that pushed Sarah into a story again, finally: a bubblegum pink '50s merry widow gifted from the trunk of a car. The car—and the merry widow—belonged to a girl Sarah met on OkCupid, Katherine. Sarah had originally contacted Katherine because Katherine said in her profile she wanted to be contacted by someone who'd play dress up and pull each other's hair, because the shape of Katherine's red mouth looked vampiric at the same time that it seemed on the verge of falling open in total submission, and because Katherine looked more like Sarah than anyone Sarah had ever seen. It was alluring to Sarah, to see someone who looked just like her lying on a pink velvet fainting couch in a lace dress reading old books full of expired plant science, or lifting the sides of her Victorian doll dress to reveal lace-top stockings.

In person, though, Katherine seemed sad and shy— apologetic, almost, for existing. Her shoulders were hunched and she stared at her cocktail, using its stirrer to swirl circles in it over and over as she gave slow, nervous answers to Sarah's questions. She wore an ankle-length floral dress and instead of looking voluptuous like in her photos, she just looked doughy. When she talked, she lifted her eyes to meet Sarah's, but her head stayed tilted toward the table.

Still, after cocktails, Katherine offered to drive Sarah home. In front of Sarah's building, Katherine opened her trunk and offered the merry widow to Sarah, saying she used to wear it at work but it no longer fit. Then she took out a bottle of Jameson and offered to come inside.

Inside, Katherine opened Sarah's refrigerator and, from between leathery unwrapped burrito halves and Tupperwares holding bluing sludge, took out a wheel of cheap Brie still in its plastic and set it down on the counter. "I like your apartment," she said.

"Sorry it's so messy," said Sarah.

Katherine shrugged. "Bukowski said that people with clean kitchens have detestable spiritual qualities."

As Katherine and Sarah swigged whiskey and talked about pop psychology, astrology, Greek mythology, the waves of feminism, and their toxic mothers, Katherine ate the Brie, knifed triangle by knifed triangle, until the entire wheel was gone. Sarah felt a little disgusted and a little like eating a whole wheel of Brie on a first date was the most liberated thing a person could do. Sarah wanted to feel liberated. She took the merry widow into the bathroom and tried it on. At the sight of Sarah in the merry widow, Katherine squealed and clapped and said Oh My God Come Here. It was like something had flipped inside Katherine, like the merry widow made things between them finally make sense. Katherine was laughing and her eyes were kind of sparkling and her hand was on Sarah's ass and then, without any kind of real notice, Katherine's hand was partly in Sarah's body and partly not, moving in a drunk and nonspecific way. In their drunk fuzz, Katherine and Sarah switched off noncommittally sticking their hands inside each other's outfits and bodies until Sarah took two steps over from the couch to her bed and passed out facedown, openmouthed.

Katherine was gone in the morning, and Sarah woke up to the merry widow rolled up next to her, smelling like pussy. She didn't know whose pussy and that grossed her out but felt exciting, too. She put it on and more or less didn't take it off for weeks. She lay on her couch and read Virginie Despentes and Angela Carter. Sarah suspected the merry widow's era didn't quite match the era of her apartment, which was full of narrow arched doorways and curio shelves, but somehow all the past decades collapsed for Sarah into one blurry pastel world in which women had wide hips and pin curls and smoked cigarettes from sleek holders. Sarah didn't use a holder but she smoked out the window after gazing at her own reflection in her laptop's Photo Booth app and masturbating to it. Smoking and masturbating were Sarah's two favorite things. In the studio apartment for which she paid her very own rent, far away from the girls with the microwave popcorn and ignoring all calls from her own parents, she was beginning to accept this.

One day Sarah opened the door to the hallway, sweating in her tutoring jeans, and taped to it was an eviction notice. She added this to the trampled garden of unpaid parking tickets and thought about what she could do that would be less exhausting than teaching children. Sarah had been fired from every job that had required her to work for more than a couple of hours in a row—barista, waitress, administrative assistant. She cried, each time, being fired, because she hated rejection and felt she was really trying, it was just that after hour three or four of being called sweetie or miss, of repeating stock phrases like haveaniceday et cetera, she'd grow exhausted and would disassociate and somehow a packed-up takeout salad would end up in the warming cabinet or a table would never get their rounds of drinks. At jobs, people always thought Sarah was stupid and she hated having people think she was stupid. But Sarah remembered Katherine had told her that she'd originally gotten the merry widow *for a job*. Katherine seemed like someone who'd disassociate, too, and so maybe the job Katherine had was something Sarah could do. Sarah was good at finding things on the internet. Sarah Googled. She found the site. She sent an email. She made an appointment.

And now she was actually leaving the house to meet with strangers in her shellacked red lips and stiff puff sleeves. Her appointment was in Hollywood and she heeded Bette Davis's advice, she took Fountain. The car was full of Sarah's garbage—smashed paper coffee cups, half-empty plastic ramekins of hardened cream cheese, tampons with unpeeling plastic wrappers and bits of debris caught in their fraying cotton. This girl in the story, in her prim dress, felt judgmental. This was *not* who *she* was *ew*. She was a clean girl. The clean girl popped in a CocoRosie CD and watched her red lips in the rearview, singing about werewolves. She gazed out the window and watched the black outlines of palm trees and glowing letters of fast food shops and furniture stores as they whisked by in the thick dusk. The city finally felt like it existed for her.

When the new Story Girl arrived at the address she was given, she felt surprised to discover that the address belonged to a house, a kind of regular-looking house, with yellow-painted panes of whatever it is houses are made of.

She pushed the doorbell with her finger. The door buzzed and she walked through it to find herself standing in a small, carpeted room with a large desk, back and center. The room could be the waiting room for a doctor, or maybe a principal's office, but from another time—there were low, purple velveteen chairs and Lucite tables and in place of *People* and *Newsweek* were magazines whose covers displayed photos of naked women with feathered bangs and furry pubic triangles. The woman behind the desk had red curly hair and a face stretched and filled in a way that reminded Sarah of a cat. She was wearing a sundress.

"Can I help you?" she asked.

"I have an appointment with Lady Lydia," said Sarah.

"Oh, good, you're adorable," the cat-faced woman said. "I'm

sick of ugly girls coming in here and crying when they don't make any money." The woman stood up and grabbed a ring of keys. "I'm Lydia," she said. "Come with me."

In a room with peach walls and a tiger-striped fainting couch, Lady Lydia told Sarah about safety rules, dress code. She handed Sarah a long list of approved and disallowed attire, protocol for greeting a client, etc. "Everything's legal here," she said. "We have extra keys to all the rooms, so scream if anyone tries anything and someone'll bust in there. We don't tolerate any shit here, none of that 'customer is always right' crap."

"That's so nice," Sarah said. She was used to being surrounded by people who tolerated a lot of shit.

"Do you have a name?" Lady Lydia asked.

Sarah did not have a name. She looked at Lady Lydia's curly orange mane and black pointy manicure. She looked at the tiger-striped fainting couch. *Lions and tigers and bears, oh my*, said something somewhere to Sarah's brain.

"Dorothy," Sarah said. It was how she felt—like she'd been dropped into an Oz.

"Dorothy's great," said Lydia. "It'll remind them of their dead wives." She stood up and placed a palm between Sarah's shoulders. "Come on baby, let's go test you out."

Sarah walked down the hall into a mirrored room with a black table in the center. The underside of the table had cabinets, like a doctor's examining table. On the back wall of the room, three girls in pastel lingerie sat on a black leather sofa with computers open in their laps. "Girls, this is Dorothy," Lady Lydia said. All the girls smiled and waved. They were all shiny bobbing ponytails, pink and blue candy manicures. "I'm Addison," one girl said. Another girl said, "I'm Roo, omg your shoes are so cute!" The third girl closed her laptop and asked sweetly, "Can we stay and watch, Mistress?"

"That's up to Dorothy."

"Sure," Sarah said. She liked being called Dorothy, liked that everyone here accepted her as a fictional character, that everyone acted as though she weren't invented two seconds ago. Lady Lydia appraised Sarah, then, like a horse. "All right, put your arms on the table and lift up your skirt, baby," she said. Sarah complied, such that her exposed ass was facing the girls on the couch. Lady Lydia hit Sarah with a leather strap, lightly and then harder and harder. Sarah thought about the phrase *testing the merchandise*, understanding that she was the merchandise. Somehow she liked this. It was better than teaching kids to read, anyway: a simple, clean transaction. Dorothy would be rented out hourly and then Sarah could go home. No plastic waste, no byproducts. No worrying about anyone's sad future. As she was hit with a leather strap, she had a memory of a random old woman, some friend of an aunt maybe, telling her she was too pretty to study so hard. Her prettiness, she realized, was how she was supposed to be supporting herself. She was finally doing things right. Little sounds of delight emerged from the shiny o-mouths of the girls on the couch each time the brand-new girl called Dorothy was hit with the strap. Maybe, Sarah thought, listening to these sounds, she'd make some friends who weren't living off microwave popcorn while spending all their energy pretending they weren't treated as merchandise.

Back at her studio apartment, Sarah picked out an outfit for the first day of work. She could wear the merry widow, she decided, after she ran into Katherine, after she made sure it was okay that she'd followed Katherine to her job. She suspected it would be. Katherine seemed lonely, like she'd welcome any kind of invasion into her life.

She decided on a short blue jumper and white ruffled ankle socks. The jumper was from a Halloween when she'd been devil with a blue dress on, a costume idea she found on the internet after finding the jumper for $5 at a thrift store. The ruffled socks came in a padded manila envelope her mom sent, full of stuff she hadn't wanted but now might. She put her hair in low pigtails. She looked like a slutty Judy Garland, she thought.

It wasn't that Sarah didn't want to be her own person, it was just that she couldn't figure out how other people became specific like they were. She wasn't sure if everyone did this, if everyone's shared secret was that they mimicked fictional characters, or if this was a personality disorder she hadn't learned about in her college psych classes. Maybe she would have learned it eventually, if she hadn't switched her major to English. Maybe she'd be, like, a mental health professional if she hadn't switched her major to English. The thought made her feel a little sick. It was easier to think you never could have been anything. Sarah lay on her couch taking selfies in her jumper and red lip goo until she felt better. She put on Blonde Redhead and jerked off in her laptop camera.

At the yellow house, Katherine wasn't there. The brand-new girl called Dorothy sat in the corner of the black leather sofa in the room called the Dressing Room. In the Dressing Room, the walls were mirrored. Sarah watched as a skinny pale and freckled girl came in wearing Converse and jeans and a ponytail and became a stilt-heeled black latex creature with slicked hair and curves and shiny red lips that looked prosthetically attached. "I'm Crow," the creature said, monotone, glancing back.

"Dorothy," said Sarah.

Crow ice-glared at her own face in the mirror and then moved her eyes a little to the side. "Dorothy looks exactly like Mabel," Crow said to someone behind her.

The someone at whom Crow was looking was Addison. Apple-cheeked and bright-eyed, twiggy in her schoolgirl outfit, Addison actually looked like a small Catholic child. "You do," Addison said, "look exactly like Mabel." Addison raised her shoulders up then and relaxed them back exhaling loudly. She repeated this motion three times, and then walked across the dressing room and back, her heels clacking slowly. "I'm learning the Alexander technique," she announced. "It's a form of postural alignment that undoes the harm we've been taught to do to our bodies."

"What kind of harm?" Sarah asked. She really wanted to know. She liked the idea of undoing harm, even if she wasn't sure that you could.

"The whole point of school is to train us into obedience. They're training us to sit in chairs for eight hours at a time," Addison said, raising her shoulders up to her ears and then relaxing them back. "Chairs fuck up our spines, which affects the health of the rest of our entire body. Simultaneously, our bodies are so stressed out by putting energy into trying to make us stop sitting, that chairs make us stupid. They teach us not to believe in our instincts."

The girl in the corner snorted. This girl was called Nadya, Sarah knew. Nadya was wearing a pink Snuggie and no makeup. She leaned back scowling with her legs spread like a dad, but she was prettier than everyone else. Her bone structure was sharp, her eyes were dark, and her skin had yellow undertones that made her not look like a sick infant rabbit without makeup, the way Addison sort of looked before she'd put lashes and a bunch of concealer and highlighter on. "I can't believe you're letting some dead asshole tell you what to do with your body," Nadya said. "I don't know who this Alexander guy is but he probably would have been one of our idiot clients if he were around now." Nadya leaned back further. "I mean, chairs are great."

Addison rolled her eyes and blinked. "Your sunny disposition is sure to make it *rain* today." She curtsied and waved like a trained showbiz toddler before turning on a heel and strutting out.

"Every week, that bitch comes in here and says her life's changed, but every week, she's still here," Nadya said. She sized Sarah up. "Dorothy, huh? What's your deal?" She raised an eyebrow. "If you're trying to find your way back to Kansas, you should try LAX." Nadya grinned like Jack Nicholson and then said, "You do look exactly like Mabel. Mabel's a fucking nut. You'll meet her."

Crow darted her eyes toward Nadya's reflection. "I don't like mental health shaming," she said.

Sarah was going to say that she might actually already know Mabel when the intercom buzzed. "Dorothy?" it said. "A gentleman would like to meet with you in the Parlour."

The Parlour was a tiny room behind a red velvet curtain. A man sat on an armchair and Sarah sat on the rug and gazed up at him, folding her hands on her knee, as she'd been instructed. She was surprised by how easy she found it to step into a wide-eyed placidity that was just a ramped-up version of what everyone seemed to expect from her already. She'd been rebelling against this placidity forever, she realized, because relaxing into it felt like weird relief.

She led the gentleman up the stairs. He was an old cowboy type who wanted Dorothy to crawl obediently across the floor with a riding crop between her teeth, to kiss his hairy toes and lay by them like a tamed animal. Sarah felt grossed out yet safe, which surprised her. Normally, she felt unsafe all the time—exposed, vulnerable, blurry. She hated leaving her apartment. But there was something amazing about everything that would happen being spelled out and transactional, about not worrying how far things would go.

She went home with $140.

Back in her building, Sarah wrote a rent check and slid it under the manager's door. It was seventy-one hours after she'd received her eviction notice. She felt miraculous. She drank a full bottle of Two-Buck Chuck and watched five episodes of *Say Yes to the Dress* in celebration. The show always made Sarah cry, the way traumatized girls hid themselves in fitting rooms until they felt confident enough to emerge, confident they'd be able to convince their families, the very people who'd made them feel like shit in the first place, that they were beautiful enough to display at a wedding. Sarah thought of her own mom crying when she'd gotten her septum pierced, staying theatrically in bed for a whole day after Sarah shaved her head. Sarah thought that if her mom could see her in her sex-work makeup and jumper, she would be happy with how Sarah looked for the first time in years.

Next time the brand-new girl called Dorothy went to the yellow house, Katherine was there, sitting on one hip in an armchair in the lobby. Katherine's face was powdered and her hair tied to the side chignonishly. She wore a sheer black lace dress with visible black panties underneath, round-toed black heels. She looked more like her internet photos in here. She looked all up in her power. Katherine stood and took Sarah's hands. "Everyone's been telling me I have a little sister here now," Katherine said. "I was hoping it was you."

"I'm so happy to see you," Sarah said.

"I'm Mabel here," Katherine said, curling one side of her upper lip like a '30s starlet.

Mabel was popular and spent most of the day sessioning, but she came back to the dressing room between clients to fix her makeup. She filled in her liquid liner, sniffed her pits, and then grabbed Sarah's wrist. "Come over after we get off work," she said. "I'll take pictures of you for the website."

At Katherine's, they worked through a twelve-pack of Tecate as they set up poses and laid out outfits: Katherine's corset and lace-top stockings, Sarah's short blue jumper, Katherine's pale green '50s wiggle-skirt dress with a waist-tie apron. Katherine gave Sarah instructions that turned her into sexpot, toddler, wife. Dorothy was regal, seductive, and languorous in a corset on the Victorian fainting couch. Dorothy was mad and bratty in her jumper, throwing her sippy cup across the kitchen and scrunching her face. Dorothy was cute, bored, and sex-starved in her apron. Katherine dumped all the photos into a folder

48

on her desktop labeled "Dorothy" and picked up a joint from
the ceramic half shell on the table, lit it, passed it to Sarah.
Sarah got stoned and then felt freaked out that she didn't
recognize the girls in the photos, that Katherine had somehow Frankensteined up these Dorothys via her closet and her
camera lens and her voice and Sarah's body. Sarah felt confused
about whether these Dorothys had always existed within her
or if Katherine was able to make the Dorothys from scratch, if
she was scratch.

Back at the yellow house, everyone squealed over the photos.
"These toddler ones are so fucked up," Nadya said, but she
laughed, looking at in-person Sarah with new respect.

Sarah was wearing her merry widow, and everyone squealed
over that, too. "It's a hand-me-down from my sister," Sarah
said, batting her eyes.

"Dorothy," Lady Lydia said, pointing with her purple acrylic
nail. "You. Are so fucking cute," she said. "I'm so glad you
found us. I fucking love you."

It felt amazing, for Dorothy to be someone who could
receive love.

Things were slow. The girls sat around complaining about dates
and ordering food from the Middle Eastern place down the
street, eating hummus and getting irritated with each other.
Katherine went to go session.

"He's not texting back," Lulu pouted, looking at her phone.
Lulu was a wannabe-photographer who favored hot pink
teddies. She was thin with long, wavy hair and a dreamy,
hopeful face.

"The old guy?" Addison asked.

"He's old, but I like him," said Lulu. "He took me to Café Montmartre two nights ago and we had a great time, and now nothing."

"He'll call," Addie said. "He's probably busy."

Nadya smiled her pumpkin smile. "Yes, he's super busy, for sure. A deep conversation with his midrange table candy from last week is definitely the very next thing on his priority list."

Lulu made a sound like a kicked shih tzu.

Katherine came in from a session in a cream vintage girdle and cone bra and pulled her hair into a ponytail. "Oh good, the food came," she said, opening a Styrofoam container and dipping a fry into a plastic container of za'atar.

Addison stared. "Mabel, I just feel like you'd be healthier if you stopped eating stuff like that," she said. "You might make more money, too."

Mabel spun toward Addie and smiled smug and glinty, pursing her burgundy lips before popping them open and shoving a fistful of fries into her mouth. She stared at Addie as she chewed, her thighs pushing at the seams of her girdle in a way that made Addie look like a skinny little twerp, and Sarah loved her.

The girls at the yellow house were way beyond abandoning The Only Story. They had boy slaves come over to do their cleaning, they were aerialists in three-way relationships, they had sex with each other after work, they didn't eat gluten or sit in chairs, they had a lot of conspiracy theories, like that the people who were running the country were all literal descendants of reptiles. Way beyond The Only Story, Sarah was noticing, logic could get freaky. Sarah felt attached to gluten, chairs, and a feeling of certainty that all humans were mammals.

The girl called Roo didn't have any new lifestyle choices or conspiracy theories to talk about, though, or if she did, these girls in the Dressing Room were not her preferred audience. She sat with big pink headphones on and ate pizza and watched *RuPaul's Drag Race*.

"I hate that fucking show," Nadya said. "When guys get all glammed up and act out stupid role-plays, they get to be famous. We do the same thing just to sit here in this hummus-and-vagina-smelling room with a bunch of whiny bitches with *theories* 'til some dude decides to show up and slobber all over our feet for a hundred bucks."

Dorothy had a session in which she pretended to be dead. The client hadn't asked for that exactly—he'd just asked her, shyly and uncomfortably, not to move, to keep her eyes closed, to yield only as much as he pushed her, but she was starting to understand what these clients wanted. This client wanted a dead girl, a girl he could bend over a table, a girl he could lay down on the zebra carpet with folded hands, whose legs he could lift like parts of a machine, like a dead girl's legs. She could be that. Each hour when the intercom buzzed to say ten minutes were remaining, he asked if it was okay to extend the session and then Dorothy would have to rouse from the dead for two seconds, long enough to say, "We'd like to extend, Mistress." Lady Lydia definitely wasn't going to let her stay dead for four hours without hearing from her. At some point, though, Sarah began to feel like she was floating just above her body. She felt like her body must have always been working so hard to resist gravity, because now her jaw sunk and her eyes retracted in her head. It was like she was more relaxed than ever before, like she was in an amniotic sac. In the end, the man handed her a hundred dollars. The desk would give her four hundred, she knew—half the amount the man paid for the four-hour session. It felt good to make five hundred dollars just from lying there. "You're amazing at this," he said. "Thank you." The man was holding her hands and looking like he might cry. Sarah felt like Jesus.

She tilted her head down and smiled up at him fake-shyly or maybe real-shyly, it was hard for her to tell what she felt.

"I have appointments with other girls tomorrow and the next day, but I'd like to see you again. I'll be back in town in October. If it's okay with you, I'm going to try to make an appointment now."

It was weird to think about October. Sarah thought about herself in the eyes of this man, as someone who would just be sitting in the dressing room, eating pastel cupcakes and waiting, until October. She wondered what level of management of the Grand Shitpile you needed to be at before you could afford to semi-regularly fly to Los Angeles to spend thousands of dollars to sate your fetish for necrophilia. Probably he talked shit about sex workers and voted Republican, which made Sarah sad to think about because besides probably wanting all women dead, he seemed really sweet.

After work, Sarah drove with her five hundred dollars to Hollywood Boulevard, where there were a couple blocks of shops that existed just for sex workers. It was amazing, Sarah felt, how whole worlds existed right beside or within the world you thought you were in. In the sex worker shops, the windows displayed tacky jewel-toned bustiers and garter belts, sheer red teddies, rhinestoned clear platforms. Sarah went into the shoe store. In the shoe store, Sarah found a pair of red sparkly Mary Janes with a six-inch heel and high toe platform, three thin straps over the top of the foot. Looking at them on her own feet in the mirror, she salivated a little. They were eighty dollars, but they'd make her money, Sarah justified. Dorothy needed red shoes.

Sarah wore her shoes all evening as she drank Tecates in her apartment. She felt sort of fascinated that she was recognized as a worker, and sort of absurdly excited to return to the yellow house. Sarah texted Katherine a photo of her shoes and Katherine wrote back with a bunch of exclamation points. Sarah wrote back, *Wanna come over and see?*

Katherine came over wearing a short floral dress with poufy sleeves and a bib. "I brought you one, too," Katherine said.

Sarah went to change into the doll dress and Katherine poured Jameson into a teacup. "So have you had any fun sessions?" Katherine asked.

"I don't know. I had one session where I was kind of... dead, I guess? It was kind of weirdly meditative to just lie there and be watched."

"Sounds easy."

"I'm mostly so resentful of the clients though. It's fucked up that they get to spill out everywhere and be so smug and pleased with themselves and meanwhile Lady Lydia's constantly yelling at me to put a corset on and checking my pits. Because *one time* I came in with pit stubble."

Katherine shrugged. "I eat whatever I want and don't shave," she said. "Lydia yells at me and all the girls are, like, grossed-out babies about my pits but I just say fuck all of them and make my money. Guys are mostly turned on by anything they think's subversive." Katherine opened a can of beer to have alongside her whiskey-tea. "Just let Dorothy be whoever she wants to be."

"I always care too much about what other people think," Sarah said.

"You need to have more fun," Katherine said. "Let's write new website copy so we can session together."

"Copy saying what?" asked Sarah.

"I'll be like, *My little sister Dorothy just came to join us! I just love to torment her. Come play with us! Watch me spank her and pull her hair!*" Katherine said. "And you can say, like, *I love my big sis Mabel but she can be soooo mean.*"

"Why are we talking like six-year-olds?" Sarah asked.

"Because our clients are disgusting," Katherine said. "Also it's really fun being six."

"What does it mean that I like being dead?" Sarah asked later, in bed.

But Katherine was already dead to the world, a strand of drool connecting her open mouth to Sarah's pillow.

The next time she was at the yellow house, the girl called Dorothy wore her red shoes and sat in the front. The front was like a pastry case. If a guy walked in and you looked cute, he might not bother making the other girls line up at all. The thing about sitting in front was you had to keep your shoes on and your corset laced, so it was uncomfortable. But Sarah enjoyed the discomfort. And it was quiet. Sarah sat on a pillow on the floor with her legs folded to the side. She opened *Story of the Eye* in front of her and pursed her lips at it. This is who Dorothy was, she decided, a perverted bookish girl. It's who Sarah was, too, but if Sarah was young, Dorothy was teenaged. Anyone coming in, she thought, would want to scoop her up and spank her, maybe even make her sit on his lap and read her dirty book aloud.

Roo walked in and screamed a queeny scream. She removed her pink headphones. "Those shoes are amaze," she said. "I want to put them in my mouth."

Sarah laughed.

"No seriously," said Roo. "Give me your foot."

Sarah raised her leg in the air. Roo hoisted it a little higher, pushing Sarah's calf. "Ow," Sarah said, giggling. Roo stretched lips around the huge platform toe portion of Sarah's foot, and then released it, leaving a pink ring. "Yummy," Roo said. "I'm a puppy sometimes but I'll only eat the best shoes." She winked and disappeared back into the dressing room. Moments like this, Sarah felt, made it worth coming to work, even if no one came in.

Sarah sat for hours without loosening her corset, leaning against chairs to support her, lying on her side. She had always enjoyed pushing herself to her physical limits, especially when no one was paying attention, and she enjoyed privately knowing that she had not taken a full breath all day long. "I'm sorry it's been so slow, baby," Lady Lydia said, later. "Look at you in that corset, you're like seventy percent ass. If this were the eighties you'd have so much money you wouldn't know what to do with it. In the eighties we all bought houses in West Hollywood, working here. That goddamn internet's turned everyone into cheap whores with those little fucking cameras, and they're ruining it for you girls."

"Houses?" Sarah said. It seemed amazing.

"Houses, cars, restaurants every night, cocaine," Lady Lydia sighed.

Lydia hit the intercom button. "Roo, are you dressed, baby?"

Roo bounded out in her magenta shoes, ponytails swinging. Roo also seemed teenaged.

"Yes, Mistress?"

"You girls want to waft?"

"Waft?" Sarah said.

"You've never wafted?" said Lydia.

"What are we wafting?" Sarah asked.

"Pussy energy," said Roo, as though it were obvious. "To attract clients."

"You guys gotta waft double strength cuz my pussy's old as fuck," said Lydia.

So Dorothy and Roo and Lady Lydia stood at the windowed door to the yellow house, wafting. Sarah liked the idea of doing this. She pictured girls everywhere, standing at their windows and wafting pussy energy into the world. That was the sad thing though—they could all waft all the pussy energy and all it would do is lure the sad old men who wanted to fuck them. Sarah wished the pussy energy could do something else.

No one came in despite the wafting, until someone did. The person who walked in had been in Sarah's Intro to Critical Theory class and now she was here, somehow, in Sarah's yellow house all the way in Los Angeles. Her name was Steele and she had a naturally silver buzz cut and eyes that looked steely, too. Sarah had always been afraid of her. Steele was the kind of girl who was angry at everyone, even the professor who Sarah felt was teaching brilliant, liberating things but who, Steele alone could see, was a smug asshole who prioritized Western thinkers and male ones. "Oh so he throws in Gayatri Spivak at the end and thinks he's so current and inclusive," Sarah remembered Steele saying while some of them were outside smoking after class. It felt awful to see Steele here, especially when Lady Lydia squealed and clapped and embraced her, when they both jumped and giggled in their embrace as though Steele was a peer.

"How was your trip, baby?" Lydia asked Steele.

"Amazing," Steele gushed. "I have a million pictures to show you."

"Did you see the adorable little girl we got while you were gone? This is Dorothy."

"I saw her on the website!" Steele said cheerily. She looked down at Sarah and pursed her lips together like she tasted something gross. "Juliana," she said, staring just a beat too long. "Gonna change, see you later, Mistress," she called, turning on a heel and strutting away. She looked as though she were walking with a book on her head.

Sarah spent the rest of the day avoiding Steele. She told Lady Lydia that her head hurt, and asked if she could read on a bed in one of the session rooms. She curled under a zebra print blanket, reading and jerking off. She was annoyed by Steele's name. Juliana was so obviously from Anne Rice's pseudonymously published Sleeping Beauty porn. Rice's Lady

Juliana was powerful and slutty, she wore pink, she liked smashing roses, and you never got to find out what was inside her brain because she didn't need to think, she had everything figured out. Sarah was trying so hard to be a *thoughtful* whore, a whore who read, a whore who *processed*. Being a whore who processed, she could see now, was like being a whore who had figured out all the government conspiracies or was learning the Alexander technique. Steele had always been smarter than her.

Back at Katherine's, Sarah complained about Steele. They'd begun going to each other's apartments after every workday. They barely discussed it anymore, just drove to one of their places and started drinking. It was hard otherwise, Sarah realized, to transition to being alone after a day at the yellow house. And it was almost impossible to transition to being with other people, people who didn't know Dorothy.

"She glared so rudely when I'd ask questions in class, like I was so dumb and suburban while she knew about cities, French theory, postcolonialism, Karl Marx."

"Were you dumb and suburban?"

"Yeah, but she didn't have to be mean about it. Anyway it just weirds me out that she's here, like, why isn't she in some, like, special program in France?"

"Did you not recognize her on the website?" Katherine asked.

"She's covering her face!" Sarah pulled up Juliana's page as evidence. Her silver hair is there, but her face is covered by her arm, a hood, a book, etc. in every photo. Still, it was so clearly Steele, Sarah realized. Sarah read Juliana's page out loud in a mocking baby voice. "I live to serve You, Sir. I know my place beneath Your feet. I am a naturally bratty girl who needs good training and I crave Your command."

"Sounds pretty basic," Katherine shrugged, going into the kitchen and spooning pad see ew into a bowl. Instead of grocery shopping, Katherine ordered large amounts of food from a Thai delivery place weekly.

"But look at her Facebook!" Sarah said. "It's all end racism, end misogyny."

"You can want to bottom and want to end structural inequality, Sarah," Katherine said. "Do you also think it's contradictory that I get beat up by men for money and want to be a therapist?"

"No, you'll be a good therapist," Sarah said. "I'd go to you."

"Aw thanks," Katherine said, looking like the shy girl Sarah first met.

"Nadya lives there, you know." Katherine raised an eyebrow and let that hang.

"That's intense," Sarah said. "So she's always Nadya."

"She's always Nadya."

In the morning, the girls slept way past the eight a.m. street cleaning, and when Sarah went out to look for her car, it was gone.

"If you have over five parking tickets, they can tow it," Katherine said.

"I have way over five parking tickets," said Sarah. "Maybe five times five. Maybe five times twelve."

"I know," Katherine said. "We can look up how much you owe online."

Katherine found instructions and looked up Sarah's situation.

Her situation was, she'd have to pay the city almost six thousand dollars, and she only had two weeks before they sold it at auction. Six thousand dollars was probably more than the car was even worth. Sarah felt like she couldn't breathe. She lay down on the floor. "I'm having a heart attack," she announced.

"Here, take an Ativan," Katherine said, taking an orange bottle from her bag and placing a pill between Sarah's lips. "You'll be okay," Katherine said. "I'll drive you to work. Just lay here while I get our stuff together." Katherine put on an old silent movie on her laptop. "Clara Bow helps me with panic," she said, pulling Sarah's head onto her lap and rubbing her scalp. "Anyway, I can't really pay my rent, so maybe I should just move in. We can be semi-lesbionic sisters who share a bed like in Victorian novels." Katherine got up then, and put a pillow under Sarah's head, started collecting shiny and lacy garments from around the apartment and stuffing them into a bag.

"Do you think our job makes us bad lesbians?" Sarah asked.

"I think it makes us great lesbians," Katherine said. "We're like *taxing* the patriarchy. And we're *ruining* our femininity."

"It's true," said Sarah. "We're unmarriageable. That's cool. I guess I just imagined we'd be taking *more* of their money. Enough to build a separatist commune and live there forever. I didn't need it to be super luxurious, I just wanted chickens and a little fruit tree orchard and at least one person I actually wanted to have sex with. I guess I had stupid dreams of never working again."

"Free porn has destroyed your dreams," Katherine said. "You could be a therapist, too?"

"No," said Sarah. "I don't want to convince anyone they should live in this stupid world."

Sarah felt like crying the whole time she was at work thinking about the loss of her car, just because she couldn't wake up in the morning to move it. She set multiple alarms and succeeded at least half the time, she figured. So much effort had gone into waking up and putting clothes on before eight a.m., getting out of the house and sitting heavy-eyed and hungover in Hollywood traffic looking desperately for a space. No one cared about this effort—she had failed overall, and now her things could be taken.

The first night after Katherine moved her stuff in, she and Sarah dyed their pubes magenta and drank three bottles of champagne out of scalloped teacups as they sat spread-eagle on the floor waiting for the bleach to take. Sarah's apartment was full of bones and fish taxidermies now, of books of expired scientific theory and Victorian chairs, Katherine's things. They hung a prism in the window so that every day at sunset, the apartment would fill with tiny rainbows. Sarah felt like she was becoming the fantasy of herself she had first imagined via Katherine's OkCupid page.

"Hi, babies," said Lady Lydia. "Mabel, one of your clients just called. He wants a sister session with you two. I scheduled him for three thirty."

Katherine dressed Sarah in some old clothes from her locker, a short ruffly lavender skirt and crop top, white knee-highs and chunky Mary Janes.

"I would have actually worn this outfit in middle school," said Sarah.

"You are in middle school," Katherine said, brushing Sarah's

61

hair up into pigtails. Katherine was wearing a skintight, low-cut purple dress that stopped just before the bottoms of her ass cheeks.

"You're a real sick fuck, Mabel," Nadya said.

"Thank you," Katherine said, tossing her hair.

"I'm obsessed with you guys," said Roo, monotone, not removing her giant headphones.

In session, Sarah clung to Katherine like a scared kid.

"When Dorothy and I were little," Mabel told the client, petting her sister's hair, "we used to love to play house. I would be the mommy and Dorothy would be the baby."

Mabel put her arm around Dorothy. Dorothy leaned into Mabel and sucked her own thumb.

"Dorothy would come home from school and I'd make her cookies and milk, only I'd tell her they were shit cookies and pee-milk and Dorothy would cry and refuse to eat them."

"You'd get so mad when I cried," Sarah said in a breathy baby voice.

"And then I'd have to punish her," Katherine said.

"You let her punish you?" the client asked.

"She was so much bigger than me," said Sarah. "Plus Mom and Dad believed whatever Mabel told them. She tricked everyone into thinking she was the perfect child. But when I was alone with her, she was cruel. She would pull my hair and threaten me, but no one ever believed me." Sarah was surprised to hear Dorothy's voice so clear and formed out of her own mouth. It was as though Dorothy already knew the secrets of her and Mabel's shared childhood.

"You wanna know a secret?" Katherine asked. "Dorothy still lets me spank her."

"Mabel, that's not *true*," Sarah said, stage-whispering and squirming.

They'd gone through this, the plan of Sarah screaming NO and running around pathetically in her six-inch Mary Janes until she was forced over Katherine's lap, skirt up.

Katherine held Sarah down and spanked her hard enough that she screamed for real.

After awhile Katherine said to the client, "She's been so good. Look at how red she is. This might even turn *purple*." Sarah loved being talked about in the third person. Katherine flipped her over then so that Sarah was sitting on her lap. She sucked her thumb and gazed at Mabel. "I have to rock her," Mabel told the client, already rocking her. "If she's really good, I let her nurse."

This was not something Sarah and Katherine had discussed, but Mabel was already rocking Dorothy, putting her own index finger over Dorothy's mouth and going "ssh ssh" and then she was singing "Hush, Little Baby." Mabel was coaxing Dorothy's head toward her own nipple, pushing the back of Dorothy's head so close that Sarah felt no choice but to suck. *If that mocking bird don't sing, momma's gonna buy you a diamond ring.* Sarah had always hated this song. She really couldn't handle the parade of expensive broken objects, the constant failed sacrifices made toward making the song's baby feel loved. She allowed herself to be nursed. Katherine, she thought, was really talented at this job.

* * *

On the way home, Katherine whimsically spent three hundred and fifty dollars on a giant crystal necklace that was supposed to draw money, and later ended up unable to pay her part of the rent. The whole apartment floor, Sarah began to notice, seemed as if someone had glue-sticked it with beer and allowed cigarette ash to fall all over it while the glue was still wet. They were throwing out plates again. On several days, Katherine called out sick, and Sarah came back from work to find her lying on the sofa in a sheer slip, full of some hallucinogenic, covered in rainbows at the golden hour. It was like a beautiful painting, an image from one of Sarah's former fantasies. There was a spookiness, though, in living inside a dream, plus there was the continued problem of too much crust. Crust in the takeout containers, crust in the crotches of her not-washed-enough panties, crust in the floor mats of her towed car. No one would pay you enough to be a beautiful painting anymore. In the fantasy version, she'd imagined everything clean, everything safe.

Sarah drove Katherine's car to work on the days she was sick. One day she stopped for a bagel on the way to work and while she was waiting in line, Lady Lydia called. "Hi, Mistress," she whispered into the phone.

"Hi, honey," said Lydia. "I want to let you know that there's a gentleman coming in an hour for a session with you and Steele. Can you be ready?"

Sarah felt sick imagining sessioning with Steele. "Can it be someone else?" Sarah asked.

"The gentleman likes pale skin," Lydia said.

*　　*　　*

Sarah and Steele painted their red lips on side by side in silence. When they went into the Parlour, the man sitting in the armchair was Sarah's necrophiliac.

"Hi!" Sarah said, hugging him. "I'm so happy to see you!"

"Good evening, Sir." Steele did a perfect curtsy and then knelt on the ground with her palms open on her knees. It was so cheesy, Sarah thought, so churchy. This guy didn't want church, he wanted dead girls. As the client explained what he wanted, Steele kept saying, "Absolutely, Sir," in this voice like she worked in HR.

In the room, Sarah and Steele knelt facing each other with their hands cuffed behind their backs. Then the man laid Steele down on a table and unhooked her hands, rehooked them so that they were resting on her lower abdomen. He hooked Sarah's wrists to the giant cross. Sarah slumped her head. He paced around the room in circles, looking. Eventually he unhooked Sarah and bent her over the spanking horse, her hair falling toward the floor. He sat Steele on the throne with her knees apart and eyes closed.

Sarah thought about Steele at the scholarship award ceremony back at school; they'd each been offered a five-thousand-dollar check during their senior year for outstanding contest essays. Their names were on little gilded plaques in the hallway, underneath all the other engraved names. What was the connection between being an excellent English major and playing dead in a lace thong and red lipstick? Sarah was kneeling against the bed with her hands in a prayer position. She felt her hair being pet, over and over, which was nice. This was her favorite client, she decided. He leaned her against a wall in the corner. She let her body slide and crumple, and he hoisted her back up, positioned her more carefully. She loved being attended to so closely, loved knowing she could fall and fall. Sarah did not feel judgmental toward this gentle human who had been forced to look at plastic magazine girls his whole life, who maybe even grew up in a house of dolls, who wanted totally docile pretty girls he could move around and pose. At least he was taking care of his shit, and she was helping, being dead for a while so some other girl didn't have to be dead forever, maybe. Sarah was saving lives.

And, she'd grown up around dolls and Photoshop, too. Who didn't want, sort of, to be plastic? If real power was unattainable, who wouldn't want to be a doll? Dolls got brushed with cute tiny combs. Dolls got dressed and held and pushed in buggies. The client folded Sarah onto her knees on the carpet. She thought about the hundreds of dollars she'd get from the session, and the hopefully hundreds more he'd tip. She'd stop at Whole Foods on the way home and pick up high-end Brie for Katherine, a baguette, gorgeous vegetables to make a soup for her sister on this day when being a still life actually paid. Sarah opened her eyes in a deathy flutter and peeked at Steele. Steele, posed over the spanking horse now, looked tense, not at all relaxed, even shaky. Uncomfortably alive. Sarah closed her eyes. She knew it, Sarah knew it—she was so much better than Steele, better than all the girls, at being dead.

EXORCISM, OR EATING MY TWIN

My twin and I met in the Midwestern college town where she lives, which is the town where I once went to college, at a fan convention for *Buffy the Vampire Slayer*. I was dressed as Faith, the bad slayer, in black leather and burgundy lips. My twin was Giles, the British librarian, in a sweater vest. Our twinship was not immediately obvious, but our mutual attraction made sense: I saw my twin as someone able to store and organize knowledge, while she saw me as complete and total eros. On *Buffy*, Giles says, blushing a little, upon meeting Faith, that "the girl has rather a lot of zest." Faith, on the other hand, doesn't seem all that taken with Giles, but that's because she's able to transcend her pretty-girl-ness via muscly and lethal fighting, so she has no need for him. I can't fight, though, or even do a pull-up, and so I need bookish knowledge to help me transcend my own pretty-girl-ness. I'm easily drawn to Giles-butches and anyway, a convention is like a hotel in a Marguerite Duras novel: it's a temporary and enclosed world where people are quick to intimacy.

How we met was, we were in the same discussion group for Buffy fanfic writers, talking about one-off episodes with non-vampire-centric plagues. I suggested that plague in Buffy had revolutionary potential, that it's through communicable illness or demonic curse that characters discover new ways of being, such as developing the pack mentality and feeding habits of hyenas or speaking exclusively and automatically through the medium of musical theater. My twin said something about how the show's core friendship group builds immunity by functioning as a kind of multi-person body. I saw this multi-person body as a potential form of revolutionary plague, though, too: "Mental health is always so measured by a person's ability to thrive independently," I explained. "But maybe independence shouldn't be the goal. Maybe we should be striving to be part of a multi-person body."

My twin nodded slowly and said, "I like that idea."

My twin's voice as it spoke was nothing like Giles's voice. It was like my voice—girlish with my same weird cadence. Our mutual interests in permeability and contagion felt a little uncanny, and as our identical voices mapped pathological routes to utopic merging, I felt my body respond. When people started to get up from their folding chairs, my twin and I neared each other with grave and darting eyes, swallowing and digging our fingernails into the dry skin of our bitten thumbs. I giggled in my nervousness; my twin blanched.

She cleared her throat. "We have really interesting overlap," she said. "I'm currently working on reclaiming parasitic lesbian relationships."

"Parasitic lesbian relationships," I echoed.

"You know, there are all these negative representations of lesbians in novels and film," she said, "where one girl is kind of a pathetic nothing who ends up taking on the style and persona of the other one, which is maybe who she wanted to be all along anyway." Her weight shifted to one foot. "I just want to claim being a parasite as a valid mode."

"Being a parasite as a valid mode," I said, my heart secretly leaping.

"You know," she said, "we all just want to live in and on each other, transforming each other and feeding off of each other. So why can't we just own that?"

Besides being Giles, my twin was finishing a PhD in English literature, and so she was skilled at saying bizarre and intimate things in understated ways that sounded sane and even professional. When she said this about lesbian parasites, my heart sent bright and rippling halos to the edges of my chest and I knew she could love me.

We stood in front of each other—me in my cat-eye liner and my twin in her Giles glasses and it was like a voice whispered my line to me and I managed to say, calmly, "I'd love to talk more. Have you had dinner?"

I will try to just be transparent and say what I am doing here: I am trying to exorcise the ghost of my twin, or else eat her. Exorcism would be better, since I try to be an ethical person and would like to leave her physical body unharmed if possible. It's only been three weeks since we've seen each other, so my twin is almost definitely alive, still. But if the exorcism fails, I am prepared for cannibalism.

So we went to dinner at a supper club. Since we were in a small Midwestern town, cocktails were two dollars and we got quickly drunk. It turned out, of course, that we'd both been solitary children, obsessed with Stephen King and Tori Amos. We'd both grown up lying on quilted girlbeds biting our cuticles and feeling an intense sense of missing, of pining for a twin.

My twin asked questions about work, which I didn't want to answer since I worked in a café and felt empty of other ambition, which, since I'd been raised by Jews, filled me with a kind of guilt. I asked my twin questions about her family and childhood, which made her clam up. She was raised by white Midwestern Protestants who found this line of questioning weird or rude. She seemed to legitimately want to author a paper together or something. I just wanted to know if she really was my twin.

We talked about the texts my twin was using for her project, about parasitic lesbian twins in *Tipping the Velvet* and *Heavenly Creatures*, and the band Sleater-Kinney, and an amazing thing happened: the supper club where we were drinking turned into a karaoke bar and without missing a beat, my twin said, "Oh, we should sing Tegan and Sara." This suggestion was very significant because Tegan and Sara are twin lesbian pop singers and so I knew then that she knew. There was just one Tegan and Sara song in the book, and my twin's hand, its cuticles bloody like mine, trembled as she wrote our names on the slip.

We kept talking until our names were called and then we were singing, and as we were singing it was like there, in the middle of this terrible fish-fry place, we were skating on an uninhabited frozen lake. It was like we had encountered the musical theater demon and could only give language to our feelings through the passionate vocalization of pop lyrics, and through the lyrics of Tegan and Sara we told each other:

All I wanna get is, a little bit closer. All I wanna know is, can you come a little closer?

When our song was over, a girl—college-aged, with bleached hair—yelled, "Ohmigod I love you guys so much!" My twin smiled a little, but didn't seem confused or anything, which indicated to me that maybe the girl's love was well-placed. As I looked at my twin, I saw we were flushed in the exact same spots and I wanted to throw my arms around her, to kiss her and cry out that we had found each other at last! But she just said, "I think that song went well." This was her academic training talking, I felt, or her Protestantism. She'd been taught not to gush.

We ordered one more drink. A gangly older man came over to the table and leaned his boozed-out face too close to my twin's face. He was slurring something about *was she a boy or a girl.* My twin was stammering and pale, so I flung my arm out in protection like a mom driving around a sharp curve. It was a new skill of mine to stare at men with sledgehammer-eyes that shattered their vision until they couldn't see us at all. "We don't want to talk to you," I said. The man backed off—literally, at first, facing us and scowling cartoonishly before turning around—and though my twin seemed rattled, I was a little glad this happened. It made it clear that our collectivity bred immunity.

My twin's parting line as I got in my Uber: "I'd love to talk more about some of our shared ideas. Send me some fan art, whatever you're working on."

One lie I now realize I have already accidentally told, as I think about the academic Protestantism of that parting line: I said we

71

pined on quilted girlbeds, but while my twin pined on a quilt, I did not. Jews make afghans, not quilts. I don't know why this is, but I hypothesize it's related to the physical comfort of afghans, or else the fact that quilts require permanence; a very long inheritance of scraps. Quilts seem uncomfortable, but I grew up wishing for one anyway, likely because time is not linear and I missed my twin.

Before I continue with my exorcism, I am going to rename my twin, so that I can stop saying "my twin." I will call her Tegan. Because my name, already, is Sarah.

After flying back to Los Angeles, I started to actually finish my fanfics, so that I would have a pretense for emailing Tegan. I wrote romantic slayer-on-slayer love-confession fic about Buffy and Faith. I wrote fic in which black magic Willow and sweet nerdy Willow are enamored of one another. I wrote fic in which Giles becomes a fierce and lethal fighter who puts on lipstick and leather and joins forces with Faith. I thought these stories would help Tegan see how we were compatible, how we could infect one another, be everything.

I'll say now that this is not what my therapist wanted for me. My therapist wanted me to move slowly, to work on healing from my borderline mother—my therapist's diagnosis, based on stories from my childhood and text messages I read aloud in session—she never gave me space to individuate, my therapist says. This makes me cry and cry because this sounds like something you're supposed to do when you're, like, five, individuate, and I am twenty-six. My therapist wants me to practice saying my name over and over in the mirror, introducing myself to myself, "Hi, I'm Sarah," but this feels too humiliating to even try so mostly I lie on my therapist's beige couch and wail and then go home and think, *What's so great about individuating anyway, what's great is having a twin*, and then I write fanfic.

My fanfic was obviously working because Tegan began writing back longer and longer emails about her feelings toward movies and art exhibits and internet scandals. I'd get the emails on my phone while walking in the parched hills above my house, which was where I was spending most of my time. I didn't want my city anymore, only Tegan. And these hills: trails wrapped around and around their bald scalps and no one was ever there except for me and crows. Whatever was going to happen to me was going to happen here, I decided, on a barren hill on my screen where information from Tegan arrived, on my screen where I typed stories to make Tegan love me, in the hills where it was okay to be an ugly animal.

One day I sat under a dead acacia and typed, *Can I visit?* Tegan responded immediately: *OMG YESSSS!!!* She'd lost some of her academic composure. At least in these emails, she was starting to twin me. A crow appeared at my feet and gazed with sage approval at my phone screen. These crows. They were my tarot.

Exorcism update: now it's just me and the crows. Sometimes there'll be a spiky purple flower that looks like plastic. The city is down below, and I can see the skyline, though in Los Angeles the skyline doesn't represent very much. This city is full of secret compounds, tunnels to a room in the lower regions of a mansion built into a hill where people are sitting on papasan chairs in three-piece suits deciding who is the voice of the future, to a swimming pool of queers in a collective psilocybin dream on a cliff's edge, to a basement in Chinatown where everyone's lying down like its kindergarten while a legendary seventy-year-old lesbian poet reads for hours, to an old warehouse where everyone is practicing dying.

I'm not interested though in thinking about all the little worlds I can't see, however magic. I'm interested only in typing to Tegan, letter after letter that I don't send. I think about putting my little parasitic mouth-claw in Tegan's brain and sucking from her, but the reality is, it's really hard to do: Tegan is a closed system, far away, her blood and brilliant ideas all coursing as they should, distant and unsuckable. So maybe Tegan is my parasite—I am the one whose brain is hijacked here, whose energy and life force has become a focused stream that can only flow toward our dead twinship.

So when I got off the plane, Tegan picked me up and drove me to her apartment in the Midwestern college town. At Tegan's apartment, there were no phone screens or karaoke or crows, no mediatory tools at all, and so we didn't know what to do. We had one beer each and talked about the flight, Tegan's house, and a recent Twitter scandal, all without touching, and then Tegan took a fitted sheet out of the linen closet and wrapped it loosely around the couch cushions.

"Sleep well," said Tegan.

"Sleep well," I said. We stood face-to-face in front of the couch. Then we hugged good night and instead of hugging and letting go, we hugged and no one let go. Instead of letting go, we both stretched our arms tighter and tighter around each other's backs. I could feel, through the front of my shirt, the outline of Tegan's body. I pulled my head back a little to see

Tegan's face, which right then looked just like my face, scared and alive, and then our faces smushed into each other, too. I took my shirt off and then tugged at the bottom of Tegan's shirt to signal to take it off, too, and then I was naked and Tegan was wearing a black binder tank and when I went to take that off, Tegan took hold of my hands and pushed me down on the bed.

Our kisses felt like extra-large tongues, like too many lips. It felt like maybe not kissing at all but like something else, like maybe eating. Tegan's breathing sounded heavy in a way that reminded me of whales and soon everything transformed into something so slick and open that I couldn't help but feel like we'd been returned to the sea. We stayed there for hours, in the promise of becoming primordial or futuristic. Eventually it felt like time for me to roll off of Tegan's body, so I did. I pulled Tegan's body into mine and spooned her. I'd always been an insomniac, but here, spooning Tegan, I fell instantly asleep and I knew the insomnia had always just been a result of missing Tegan, of my body's innate need to know where she was.

I want to check in about how this exorcism is going. It is going well, but for all the wrong reasons, I know. I am remembering that Tegan is my love, my only, my twin. I hear her in my heart, which beats loudly, which sounds like Te-gan-Te-gan. What I'm experiencing, I now realize, might be the opposite of an exorcism, a kind of endless feeding on memories and dreams. I fill my bathtub with hot water and gloss my lips. I climb in and roll like an eel.

*   *   *

So the next day, all sex-bonded, we strolled around Tegan's neighborhood holding hands. We walked into a rockabilly-looking haircut place with turquoise chairs and a glittery counter because the design lured me and I chose to understand this luring as *a call* and I got my hair cut. I had my hair shaved on the underside like Tegan's, but left it longer on top. The buzz of the shaver sounded violent and I liked that, something menacing in being unmade.

After the haircut, Tegan and I bought sweaters at a thrift store and then went to a grocery store to pick up beer to drink on the porch. This was a college town in the Midwest so there were many kinds of beers stacked in the fridge but Tegan pointed to a six-pack, grinning. I looked at the label on the packaging. Swirly caps spelled out TWO WOMEN. Both women were drawn with long wavy hair. One had on a German barmaid outfit with lederhosen and the other was a hippie festival chick holding a bunch of loose wheat over her boobs. I looked at myself in my black romper and combat boots and then at Tegan in her muscle tee and skinny jeans—at our shaved-and-choppy hair—and back at the two women on the bottle. They made me feel like *two women* had a kind of magic power, like maybe they were each constructed by the patriarchal gaze, sure, but here on the beer label they lived together and could be anything. I imagined them doing that barn dance where you link arms and swing around, hay flying until the hippie chick's tits were swinging free in the balmy country air. I smiled a lot. Tegan was already smiling a lot.

Back at Tegan's, I couldn't stop touching my head. I'd run my whole palm from my shaved nape upward, and then do the same to Tegan's. Feeling my head made me think that I

76

wouldn't be able to show up back in my hometown now without my mom bursting into tears and my dad yelling red-faced.
Touching my head made me think that I didn't belong to them
anymore, though, that who I belonged to now was Tegan.

Exorcism update: so, fine, maybe our twinship was always
kind of pathological. Maybe only something communicable
or demonic permitted us to speak our feelings through pop
music to begin with. I feel okay with that though. I thought
Tegan felt okay with that. I feel sick. I want to be sick with
Tegan, which would make me *not* sick, which would just make
me part of a different dimension. But a person in a different
dimension alone is a sick person, I know, and I don't want to
be a sick person. I think about how ONE WOMAN would be
a very sad beer.

So after that first visit, I wrote an email suggesting to Tegan
that I come out and live with her during winter break,
when, I knew from internet research, she had six weeks off.
During the hours that Tegan didn't respond, I refreshed my
email constantly. Each time I didn't see Tegan's name, I felt
panicked.

But then Tegan responded. *You're welcome to stay. I'll empty
the guest room closet so you can keep your things in there. I work
in the day, and sometimes at night.*

Tegan's lack of enthusiasm unsettled me, but I decided
to take any kind of yes for an answer. I quit my café job,
figuring if I did ever return, I could just find a new one. I
sublet my apartment, and flew out to Tegan's college town.
In Tegan's town, in Tegan's house, I bleached our hair, and

then palmed blue dye all over our heads with plastic gloves. I wanted us to celebrate our having nowhere to be for six whole weeks. I wanted us to achieve other-dimensionality or become a multi-person body via our collective hairdo. I put on extra sets of Tegan's shapewear and we slid back and forth on each other's bodies, listening to the microfiber zip against itself. I ordered us animal tail butt plugs from Amazon and when they arrived, Tegan admitted to having always wanted to wear one of these and we wore them—big fluffy skunk tails affixed with cylindrical rubber stoppers—as we washed dishes and watched YouTube. I knew this wasn't the exact kind of play they were intended for but I wanted us to be twin blue-haired skunks, unfit for anywhere but here.

While Tegan applied for academic jobs at the kitchen table, I lay in bed and wrote fanfic in which Dark Willow chains Nerdy Willow to the computer in the Sunnydale library and forces her to research spells to bind their souls across dimensions forever while she pulls Nerdy Willow's hair and licks her body. I wrote fic in which the two Slayers become one two-faced Slayer, a gorgeous muscled girl with all the sexual prowess of Faith and the loyalty and clearheadedness of Buffy. I wanted to bring Tegan's theories to life, to create a multi-person body with *powers*, to illustrate the magic, instead of the pathology, of the lesbian merge.

When I walked into the room where Tegan was writing, Tegan did not look up. Once, I lingered, stretched out on the bed and yawned loudly. Tegan looked back at me, shifting uncomfortably. "I'm working now," Tegan said.

When I sat on Tegan's lap and threw my arms around her neck seductively she said, "Sar, come on."

Still, at night, when we spooned on her quilt, Tegan said, "There are MFA programs here."

"I don't think my fanfic's fancy enough for that," I responded.

"Your fanfic's good," Tegan said.

And since Tegan was almost finished with a PhD, I believed her, and since all of life felt stupid except for Tegan, I started working on my application. As I wrote, I felt the lure of formation, of becoming all these things: a writer, a person in an MFA program, Tegan's *partner*. I imagined Tegan introducing me at a party: this is my *partner Sarah*, she's getting her MFA, she's a writer. We could be in the world, a little bit, protected by being a two-person body, and then go back to our private world, at home.

Exorcism update: Tegan knew then. She knew that she wanted to untwin me, and she still fed my fantasies of twinship. I sit up in bed and take deep breaths, counting to five on the inhale and seven on the exhale, like if I push out more than I take in then part of what I push out has to be Tegan. This doesn't work at all so I open my laptop and order Come To Me candles from a botanica with an Amazon store. Their impending arrival soothes me—I'll just have to wait forty-eight hours before I can cast a spell that will bring Tegan back. In the meantime I climb into the bathtub, fill it with bubbles that claim to be *calming*, and wait.

I want to talk about how cold it was there, in the small Midwestern town. It was so cold, unimaginably cold if you haven't experienced it but maybe even if you have—it caused a feeling so extreme your body probably has to forget it to even go on living. So after we walked the two blocks to the Laotian restaurant, we were red and shrunken, sweating in our thermals the second we stepped into the heated restaurant.

I looked at the menu and wanted all the words on it: pumpkin, fried tofu, pineapple, tamarind, peanut sauce. I wanted curry and noodles and sticky rice and soup. I rattled off menu items I felt excited about but Tegan interrupted.

"You should get what you like," Tegan said. "I'm just going to get chicken fried rice."

I stared. This information stung my already stinging face. I felt like, how could my twin be someone not excited to get down on everything spicy and saucy and fried, especially in this weather? I felt like, who *is* Tegan? I felt like, *chicken fried rice?*

I ordered a cocktail. Tegan said she just wanted water. Maybe she was sick.

"Are you feeling okay?"

"Yes, why?"

"Oh, I don't know, I thought chicken fried rice and water seemed...very *Franny*."

Tegan's features seemed to get smaller and closer together as her face expanded and reddened. "Well Salinger's a misogynist asshole," Tegan said.

It seemed beside the point. Even if that were true, it was also true that when Franny ordered her chicken sandwich, she was quietly rejecting the world, and more significantly, her date.

My cocktail arrived bright blue in a tulip glass.

We toasted, my cocktail and Tegan's water, and said a cheers as fake-bright as my drink and then started talking about other fanfic writers in our extended community: whose writing was amazing, who was rude at a convention once. We disagreed with each other a lot, maybe because we were both irritated about the chicken fried rice.

But then we agreed on someone who was smart, gorgeous, super nice, whose work was amazing and then Tegan said, "So, I've actually been meaning to ask, are you romantic or sexual with anyone else, like, back in your city?"

Our plates came then, landing all over the place on the table so that I had to pass Tegan her plate of rice. I felt like screaming *Of course not, um, hello, I have finally found my one-and-only!* but instead I just said, "No, are you?"

"Not right now," Tegan said. "It's kind of hard here, there just aren't that many queer people."

"Right," I said. "You wish there were more queer people here...so you could date them?"

"Well yeah," Tegan said. "I mean, I love this," she gestured, waving a chopstick back and forth between us, "but I think it's important to also see people who live near us. I didn't know how you would feel about that."

I pushed holes through a piece of kabocha squash with my chopstick. How I felt was, my heart shrunk to walnut size, like a scared snail, like a cold testicle, like I don't know, something that shrinks very fast in response to a frightening stimulus.

"For me, it's a way I can keep healthy boundaries," said Tegan. "Plus, I'm becoming aware that I crave intimacy with butches and transmasculine people."

The chunk of kabocha was full of holes and I was now using the side of my chopstick to flatten it into a paste. "Well, I'm so glad you're sharing this with me," I said. I said this not because it was in any way true but because interacting with Tegan had given me some training in Protestant academic composure, because it seemed like the right answer. "I totally want for us to be able to continue to learn things about ourselves and share them," I said. I thought, I was not attached to having any particular style of clothes or way of walking or vocal cadence; I could learn to be butch if that's what Tegan wanted.

"That's great," Tegan said. "Because I also wanted to let you know that I plan to start taking testosterone. I have an appointment for blood work next week."

"Oh wow," I said. "That's so great for you. I mean, Mazel Tov." I wanted to say the right thing, the thing that acknowledged that for Tegan our twinship no longer mattered, that we needed to respect each other as separate entities who were free to just *realize* things about ourselves and our desires, things that meant we were going to become things that were not *each other.*

"I mean if you have any questions," Tegan said. "I'm happy to answer them."

I sucked on the straw of my blue drink, pulled my security lip gloss out of my tote. Ugh, I was never going to be butch. "Well, I guess, like, why?" I asked.

"I just want to," Tegan said. "I think I'll look better, more how I want to look."

"But you look really great now," I said.

Tegan's face was very white with eyes that were somehow both buggy and retracted.

"I'll get this," said Tegan, picking up the check from the table.

"Why?" I asked. Tegan normally liked to split things down to the cent, in an embarrassing, itemized way.

"Out of generosity," said Tegan.

* * *

That night while I spooned Tegan, I thought about all the other people she might want to be spooning her. Butches and transmasculine people. The longer I held Tegan and the longer I couldn't sleep, the more I imagined Tegan's body growing hair and muscle definition, and the more I panicked. Around seven a.m. was when I realized Tegan's voice would drop, become a different kind of voice from my voice, that Tegan was going to be reborn new and I was just going to be some twinless girl.

I shook Tegan awake. I'm sure I was spiral-eyed, with some crazy up-all-night look. "How sure are you that you're doing this?"

Tegan just stared at me in a way where her entire face looked like a throat-lump.

Then Tegan got up and started making breakfast, loudly, in the kitchen.

"It's seven a.m.!" I yelled. "It's the middle of the night!"

I felt terror, terror like I had made Tegan go away forever. I lay in bed panicking for an hour and then I got up.

"So, should I use different pronouns for you now?" I asked, standing on one foot in the kitchen (*how would I ever be butch?*), my hand deep in a bag of bagel chips. At the kitchen table, Tegan looked up from writing, obviously not finding me cute at all.

"They/them," Tegan said, and looked back at their computer screen.

Exorcism update: I want to tell Tegan I'm sorry. I was unloving. Tegan is a separate person. My therapist says so and now without Tegan I have to trust my therapist. My therapist is okay.

She's trying to convince me that Tegan has never been my twin but is a separate person in the world with no inherent similarity to me, genetic or otherwise. I can admit now that Tegan is a separate person, and that I have triggered that separate person with my fear, with my bad, panicked reaction.

"Why do you think you were so worried about Tegan's transition anyway?" There is a long silence where my therapist sits, waiting for me, her eyebrows in their normal places but her eyes, somehow, cocked.

"I'm afraid of Tegan becoming someone who doesn't need me anymore," I say finally.

My therapist nods compassionately. "Why wouldn't Tegan need you anymore?"

"I guess because they'll be, like, more advanced. Like, if you're not some gross girl why would you want to date some gross girl?"

"I want to return to why you think girls are gross," my therapist says, "but I also want to point out that many, many people date women who are not, themselves, women."

"Exactly! In every relationship I've had with men, I always had to be the girl, and I felt like with Tegan I didn't have to be the girl, like, I could be something else."

"Like a different gender?"

"No, like, a dolphin...I don't know. Like it felt like there was an unspoken acknowledgment between us that every way society defines girls is horrible and so we'd have to be another kind of thing."

"Let's sit with that," she says. "Has Tegan indicated that they expect you to be more of a girl, now that they're transitioning?"

I blow my nose. "No," I admit.

"And what does it mean, to be the girl?"

All the mornings after the night of the Laotian restaurant, Tegan was up way before me typing at the kitchen table. They barely looked up as I came in and ate cool eggs from the pan on the stove. Outside, snow kept blowing at a gazillion miles an hour so that the whole world was made of dense and swiftly moving white flakes. We were stuck firmly in the house. This was the reason Tegan's winter break was so long in the first place—all of January, you couldn't go outside.

I stayed in Tegan's bed in my footy pajamas while they put on a feminist T-shirt and a cardigan and flannel pajama pants and stayed upright all day. I wrote fanfic there, which was the only way I could process my feelings, since Tegan was more and more closed off. I wrote from the perspective of Angel, Spike, Harmony. There were so many different reasons someone might want to eat someone else.

I wanted Tegan to say it was okay, that this was hard and confusing for me, so I hung around the kitchen while Tegan wrote, pretending to clean, but they didn't say that, or anything. Tegan just sighed a lot, pressed their teeth together hard enough that I could see.

One day though, Tegan looked up from sighing and said, "There's an open mic tomorrow night at a bar. I thought we could go read our fanfic." I was excited that Tegan wanted to do something together.

We parked the car and ran through the winds that hurled snow at our faces. Inside the bar, everyone who wasn't us was a white dude with a guitar and during each song about

85

bland male feelings, Tegan and I sat stiffly next to each other, unable to say anything. No one told us that they loved us or even talked to us at all and I felt like we were no longer twins, just gross lesbians, just the only non-dudes, except that soon Tegan would be a dude and I would be stranded on the island of gross lesbianism alone. Or I guess I would become a straight girl, which would be even worse. When one of the blond guitar boys approached our table to compliment our fanfic (he said "you guys" but looked only at me), I mussed my hair with my hand and made eyes at him and for maybe five whole minutes. I laughed at every boring thing he said and for a full two days after that, Tegan basically ignored me, scooting to the other end of the bed when I'd try to spoon. In the middle of the night I'd wake up to find the bed empty.

One morning, Tegan woke up to find me standing over the mattress on the floor of the guest room watching them sleep.

"Hi," I said sadly.

What Tegan said next was, "You, Sarah, are actually incapable of giving a person space. You seem to not need any space at all."

Exorcism check-in: fuck Tegan. Space was never what we agreed to. I mean, I know we only talked about things in mediated ways, but hadn't we agreed to be diseased? Wasn't that the entirety of our "overlap" that Tegan had so professionally expressed? Tegan wanted this, Tegan said yes, I felt our twinning, I had a twin, Tegan had a twin, Tegan was my twin and it was the best thing to ever happen to either of us. I light the Come To Me candles. I know you're only supposed to do one, but I put a half circle of them around my bed. I want to make sure they work. I say my prayer: *All I wanna know is, can you come a little closer.*

"Do you want me to go?" I finally asked Tegan.

Tegan didn't say anything for several minutes. My stomach felt like it was floating in the center of my body.

Then at some point, like years later, Tegan said, "Yeah."

Then Tegan said, "Sorry."

I felt calm, to have the issue finally settled. I walked through the snow to get Laotian noodles. As I lifted noodles to my mouth with one hand, I used the other to book a flight home on my phone.

I never cried. I only returned to my fanfic, to the crows. I felt severed, twinless, insomniac again. It was fine.

Exorcism check-in: I want to banish Tegan from my body—I am ready for you to stop haunting me, Tegan!—but also, I want to video-chat them, to write them a letter, or a fanfic, something that could convince Tegan that I am good, that we are good together.

I write Tegan an email and another one and another one and I send some of them, sort of at random, whenever I can't stop myself.

At night I feel my thighs thick and sticky. I feel the bulge of my belly, my tits. I feel disgusting. I hyperventilate.

In the day my voice seems like a stupid ditz voice.

In the day my voice seems like the best voice, like Tegan's an idiot for wanting to abandon this voice, like they're going to regret it.

At night I imagine Tegan bald and mad at me.

At night I check my fanfic page views and they are high and I think about how Tegan was the one who made me start actually finishing and posting fanfic at all and this makes me cry.

At night I imagine spooning Tegan and I think who cares if Tegan is a boy.

In the day I shave my head. I take a pair of clippers and set it to two, let all my hair fall to the floor.

In the day I find a gym and start lifting weights. I can twin Tegan.

In the day I get into the MFA program. It is like something out of a dream, something I never imagined could happen. It's fully funded. They give me a stipend.

At night I think about being there, in the Midwestern college town where Tegan lives, about watching Tegan get a new face, new name, new voice. I think about wanting to spoon Tegan.

In the day I email Tegan and tell them I've gotten into the program and ask could we talk. Tegan responds days later.

Congratulations on the acceptance! Tegan's email begins. They're back to being a Protestant academic. Tegan says right now it's best for them if they *continue to take space* from me, but that they wish me the *best of luck on the decision.*

At night I want to kill Tegan. I want to grab fistfuls of Tegan's growing shoulder muscles and shove them bloody in my mouth. I want to chew on Tegan's brawn.

In the day I cry and cry. I think about MFA programs. I think about the yellow hills and crows. Both feel impossibly far. I ignore the acceptance letter all together, and the institutional emails that follow.

In the day I stop waking up. It is too sunny in my city and more and more my head pounds in response to the sun, my eyes throb and feel like they will burn out of my skull.

This exorcism is not working. I thought I'd come to realize something new but all I realize is that I love Tegan. I love my memory of Tegan, or my invention of Tegan, and I hate the new Tegan, the real Tegan, who is probably not even named Tegan anymore, or rather, what Tegan was named before I named them Tegan.

In my fanfic, Angel can't bear to live around a Buffy he can't touch, but he doesn't want a vampire version of Buffy and so he eats her whole, entirely, blood first and then, sinking his face hungrily into her chest, he bites, hard, through skin, through meat, chewing on muscle fibers, tearing through veins, colliding teeth with breastplate until his lips reach her heart, which spurts and pulsates, as hearts in all good fanfic do. Meat between his teeth, Angel internalizes Buffy's fighting prowess, her wit. His teeth keep gnashing.

The fic is working for now.

I can see that cannibalism is way more fun than an exorcism could be, that cannibalism might be able to prevent having to continue this exorcism, which is starting to bore me. I put on purple lipstick and hoop earrings, which look great with my shaved head. I pull on a binder of Not-Tegan's I stole and a tank, a little leather jacket, skinny jeans, platform boots. I look at myself in the mirror and feel hot for the first time in forever.

I purse my lips at the mirror and snarl. "Hi, I'm Sarah," I say seductively. I dance a little in the mirror and feel so into my reflection that it makes me laugh. I grab my wallet and my keys. I lock the door behind me and drive, hungry, into the night.

DREAM PALACE

Now you are Sarah. Here you go, driving down the highway, short shorts riding up, thick thighs spread and sweaty on the leather of the driver's seat. It's the desert but not the gorgeous rocky kind. Instead it's the all-tan kind, barren except for some dinky brush. You're covered in a layer of grease from when you force opened your tin of lip balm and, melted to liquid, it splashed all over you. Now you feel like a plump and juicy bird, like your skin might bubble up crisp. Your AC broke, and you're pouring water all over yourself every two minutes. Your lipstick is bubblegum pink and you're wearing sunglasses. Your CD keeps skipping and you can't get a signal out here in the desert, radio or cell. You're running away, untethered, a girl and her car and a thousand dollars you've saved from tips. You want to start over you think and why not do it this way. Occasionally, you pass signs for fireworks, guns, porn, and then hours of emptiness, a single cactus, a bunch of sand.

You see a sign that says DREAM PALACE. The sign is

connected to an enormous building, a building that is like a superstore or a mini-mall covered in silver tinsel fringe.

You love palaces, and dreams.

You walk and walk around the building but you don't see a door. It looks like the entire building's been gift-wrapped, and so maybe if there is a door it's covered up. You're convinced the building's shininess is reflecting the sun back at you so you're getting it double-strength and also your thighs are rubbing together and chafing and right when it feels like they might actually bleed and you can't take it anymore you see a place where the wall ripples into what looks like steps, leading to two inflated bubbles nestled against one another. You take a swig of water and then climb, pleased to see finger notches in each of the ripples, making you feel safe, like this is the right way to do things. When you get to the top, the bubbles are touching but, instinctually, you hurl your head against the crack between them. The bubbles do not open for you. You try again. On the second head-hurl, you're sucked between the bubbles by some kind of slurpy force and thank god for your lip balm spill plus all the sweat because once you break through, you slide right in. Only now you're stuck. You're in a tight cavity just a bit larger than your body with red walls that look layered and tissuey and alive. You feel around you, and the walls are soft with little bumpy protrusions. You realize you've done it: you've made it back inside the womb. You feel both comforted and turned on even though you don't know how you'll ever get out. You want to be naked in the womb so you work to get your shorts off and then push your crotch against a bumpy protrusion which, you're surprised to find, responds as you push against it, kind of swaying against and into you. You think of the stuff that lives

92

at the bottom of the sea, the stuff that might be agentive or might just be landscape. Everything kind of sways and pulsates around you, and you're swaying and pulsating, too.

Time stops. It might be minutes or days that you're just suspended, pulsing. One of the algal protrusions extends and lengthens, undulating toward you until it nabs you in the belly button. You have a deep innie and it's a little jarring as the protrusion burrows and then roots, but also it feels good to be connected to the swaying pulsating space around you, to look down and see your skin turn into something that looks like a red seaplant or mammalian tissue. It feels good to be connected completely to this pulsing world. All thinking has ceased but you sometimes see images: a tutu-ed alligator, a swirling galaxy, a rocking horse with your mom's face.

When the womb opens, you're sure you have become something else. Whatever is now you is pushed along down a membranous pink slide, still tight and pulsing. The algal finger you're connected to comes with you, a thick eel now, which you wrap your limbs around.

You and your eel slide into a chamber where and in the chamber are two nestled girls with thick thighs and cat heads. They're fetal and head to foot. This chamber is made of plush red-velvet-sofa material, ruched and gathered with hunks of rose quartz, cushion all the way around. When you slide in, the girls unnestle and immediately home in on your navel. They lick their lips and lunge forward. One digs with both sets of claws as the other kind of butts her head into where eel meets belly and sucks. It hurts, but it feels so precise and hungry that it's like it's *what's supposed to happen* and you surrender to it. Anyway you know how birth works—you can't keep your eel

93

forever even if you might wish to. "You will stay in the Sucking Chamber three days," one cat girl whispers in a German accent once you are loose. You look down and see a green-black iridescent hole at your center. The other cat girl is still licking it clean, gathering the last loose bits of iridescence with her rough tongue. She butts her head against you, rubbing it along the length of your body. She purrs. Everyone purrs, including you. The girls keep licking you, prodding everywhere with what you understand now are paw pads. They push and sometimes claw you, drawing blood. You grab at their bellies when you're in pain from the claws and they push sweetly at yours. The girls have human mouths and several rows of human tits shaped like balloons and little cones and droopy tubes. You suck all of them. Some release something like a smoothie that tastes of banana and salt. Others contain something like a lollipop liqueur that sends your mind floating on a pink sea. Others are filled with something like seawater. You think *I am being primordial* and then you don't think at all, you are just sucking at the sea-smoothie and feeling blurred. At the end of what you guess is three days, the girls bathe you completely with their cat tongues and push you on your way.

WHOOSH you slide and slide straight into a chamber that is a room and in the room you can only crawl on the scuffed wood floor. You are surrounded by flat leather slippers, neat ankles, billowing coral skirts. You hear high-pitched laughter and tinkly clicks of glasses above. You want a glass but you can't stand, you realize. You plop down fetal and suck your thumb. Doing so, you collide with an ankle. A redheaded face appears next to the ankle and says "googoogoo" and "coochie coo" and tickles you. Someone with a severe bob bends then and scoops you. "What are you doing down here?" she shouts. "This is not where you're supposed to be." They toss you over their arm and spank you before carrying you to a dark pulsing opening that swallows you.

You're pushed along in a controlled, muscle-y, intestinal-feeling way with putrid liquid sloshing around you until you're crawling down industrial carpet, slowly growing as you crawl and then walk. The hallway smells like mildew. You walk into a room with dingy once-white kindergarten tile and computer parts everywhere. A tall, long-haired butch turns around. "Hey slut," she says. You're immediately turned on. What's weird, you realize, is this is the class bully from your elementary school, grown up. She grabs you by both straps of your sports bra and wraps her fingers around your throat as she jams her other hand down your shorts. You're super happy about this turn of events. She shoves her fingers in you and as she fucks you, she keeps holding you around the throat. When she drops her pants you're confused by her cock because you feel sure she didn't have one as a kid when she peed on you at recess. "Where'd you get it?" you whisper. "That kid in our class who died left it to me in his will," she explains. "He was a feminist, it turned out." She flips you over then, into a crouching position on the desk covered with wires and old computer parts. "Why?" she says, "You want one?" and then she laughs and laughs. She uses the wires to secure your hands and then fucks you. It seems like days that she fucks you and also too soon when she pulls out and demands, "Crawl." You crawl back down the mildewy industrial carpet hallway while the elementary school bully hits you with a riding crop and cackles, and then at the end, drops you down a sterile-seeming hole, a laundry chute.

You fall and fall down the chute like you're falling in space and it's dark and a little scary but stardust swirls in the pitch black around you and two giant slugs in space suits grab you under your arms and you swirl slow, too. Somehow you feel relaxed.

You're set gently on an operating table and what look like cartoon aliens in surgeon masks unzip your belly (which is now a kind of semi-translucent jelly material) and remove a similarly semi-translucent jelly goat, a burgundy leather pump, and a thrashing iridescent fish with smooching red cartoon lips. You're placed on a stretcher and wheeled through total darkness. The wheeling's fast and it makes you nervous and you're going up up up until eventually you're in a white airy room, a room that is breathing. There's a high, vaulted ceiling and wood beams and plush pastel objects everywhere—throws and poufs and pillows, lots of knitted things. It smells like lemon balm, sage. Your ex is on the bed under patched and patterned blankets. "Hi," you say. "Hi," they say. You crawl under the blankets. You're both wearing white cotton gowns like it's the hospital or you're babies or in *Peter Pan*. As the room breathes around you, you start breathing in sync with it and therefore with each other. You feel like twins in an incubator and you think, my ex is so beautiful and then after hours or days they just look neutral, like any other person. "I have to go now," you say and you notice for the first time that one of the knit things around you is a pair of touching knit bubbles against the wall. You walk over to it, push your body easily inside its knitted chamber, grab onto some handles, and whoosh down a metal slide, straight to your car. You get in and know exactly where you want to go.

THE FIRST SARAH

The first Sarah wore her dark curly hair loose to the waist and when she spun, it caught wind and became a parachute of hair, buoyant and rippling. This is how she looked when Abey first fell in love with her, mid-spin, gawping up at an outstretched tree limb, fuchsia petals raining down: a vision. Sarah wasn't even called Sarah yet; she was still going by her birth name Sarai, but that name's warrior vibes didn't suit her and so mostly everyone just called her Sari.

Abey and Sari shared a daddy and so Abey had of course known Sari since she was a born, but as a child, Sari had been dressed in little pants and a kippah and her curls were shorn except payos. Abey had been off studying and when he returned after many years, Sari had grown from an unremarkable boy into a beautiful girl, which is why Abey didn't recognize his half sibling spinning under the flower tree; he simply thought, this spinning girl will be my wife.

Sari was from before God created the gender binary. We

know: in all the paintings, everyone's got perfect dicks and muscles or else curves and neat slits, but that's not how it was. How it was was genitalia could look budlike or bloomed, zucchini-ish or more like a berry cluster, like an anemone or a starfish or a pair of sea cucumbers. Bodies came in all different combinations of planar and bumpy. People identified with masculine or feminine dress in ways that matched their genitalia and body type or in ways that did not and no one was mad about it yet.

Sari had genitalia like a young summer squash and Abey like an overripe zucchini, and while this was perhaps not the most common combination of genitalia for a couple in love to have, it was also no big deal. They married.

It was strange, Sari thought, that girls' joy in their own freedom was so often the thing that made men want to turn them into wives. Sari wasn't particularly itching to get married, but she knew it was inevitable and Abey was a nice boy and her mother approved, which Sari cared about. It wasn't a big deal to marry your half brother in those times; there just weren't enough people on earth for people to start getting picky about incest.

Sari was so pretty, and she delighted in the world around her, making Abey delight in it, too. Sari and Abey honeymooned for years, wandering through the desert enjoying the feel of sun on their skin. They scooped up sand and let it run sparkling through their fingers. They sliced cactuses and grilled them on a fire and fed these sliced, grilled cactuses to each other under the stars. Sari pulled her legs into the air and Abey hardened seeing the little pink star between Sari's cheeks and he pushed Sari's knees behind her ears and Sari's hamstrings smarted so good and she gasped in pleasure and Abey entered her and she felt so full so full. Abey and Sari pushed their fingers, then their squashy parts into each other's mouths and fell asleep in a dreamy layer of cum and slobber and glittery sand. They rode camels and located constellational shapes the stars made—cacti and castles and clouds. Abey and Sari were the first charters of stars.

Eventually Abey and Sari returned from their outdoorsy adventures. It was time for them to settle down. Their father said so, and so did God. They couldn't spend their whole lives traipsing around and plucking fruit off trees and coming all over each other; they were Special, or at least Abey was—he was destined, God told him, to be the father of many nations. This confounded Sari a little—how was she going to give birth to the many nations?—but Abey kept insisting that God was going to do a miracle. Sari believed Abey—God did miracles around them all the time. Plus, anatomy wasn't totally figured out yet and so no one quite knew what internal compartments babies grew in and so Sari and Abey had a different sense than we do of what is possible. They just knew that external holes connected mysteriously to internal tubes and chambers and so it seemed not impossible that a tiny baby could take root in one of Sari's chambers. Sari had a rounded little belly and at least one non-mouth hole from which outside things could enter into and emerge from the belly, transformed, and that seemed like maybe enough.

So Sari and Abey moved into a nice house with cool stone floors and thick braided rugs and abundant fruit trees and animals. They had servants to scrub the floors and bring fresh water and tend to the animals and help with cooking—Sari liked to cook still; transforming bits of the land into something edible brought her joy.

Sari loved the idea of getting pregnant. The truth was, after a couple years, she was feeling restless inside this settled life. Abey went to work, and Sari stayed home and lounged and cooked a little and felt like each day had too many hours. A baby, she thought, would give her reason to explore again—to sing, to traipse, to whirl, to pluck fruit from trees. She'd visit Abey's room in the creamiest and silkiest of nighties and cat-pose on the bed or pull her knees to her chest and purse her lips seductively. After Abey finished, she'd put her feet up on the wall in Abey's room as Abey davened and chanted his Baruch atahs.

But the davening never worked. No child rooted in Sari's mysterious internal chambers. Abey grew increasingly frustrated. He ate too much cake and drank too much wine and slept poorly. He resented Sari for being an impediment to his destiny. "I'm supposed to father many nations," he whined.

"What does God say, babe?" Sari asked, as sweetly as possible, rubbing Abey's back.

"I'll talk to 'im," Abey said, macho-ly.

Meanwhile, it was winter and the rains never came. The land grew fallow. Wheat never sprouted, leafy greens shriveled up yellow just as soon as they appeared.

The sheep were growing sick and thin and the dried grain used for chicken feed was running out. Sari was frying eggs the servants had brought from the chicken coop when Abey came into the kitchen.

"I talked to God," Abey announced.

"Oh yeah, what'd he say, hon?" Sari asked, flipping an egg.

"He says we should go south into Egypt, where we can stock up."

"What does that mean, stock up?" Sari asked, plating their food.

"I'm not sure," said Abey. "Anyway, a trip would be nice."

"I think so, too," Sari said.

Camels pulled the wagon that led Abey and Sari south to Egypt. On the wagon, the sun shone all over them. Sari sat behind Abey, straddling his back with her long naked legs as he drove, kissing sweat off his bare shoulders. The sun beat down; their bodies slipped and glistened. At night, Sari made a fire and Abey cooked potatoes and goose over it and later at night Sari and Abey gazed at the tiny tiny stars in the dark dark sky and Sari said, "I see a deer's head" and Abey said "I see it, too," and even later at night Sari draped her body over the hump of a sleepy camel and glanced seductively back at Abey; Abey slid into her from behind and held her hips and pushed like he was trying to live inside her body. In the nights of their desert travel, no one thought about babies or their legacy or the future nations and their love felt fresh again.

In Egypt, Sari and Abey were received at the palace of a king. "I'm Abey and this is my sister Sari," Abey said. He didn't know why he introduced Sari as his sister. It wasn't untrue, but it seemed it should be more true that Sari was his wife. He wondered whether "wife" made her seem too much like property in his mind, if "sister" cast her as a separate and equalish individual. Somehow, he realized, he liked better to think of them as brother and sister than as husband and wife. "We are in a famine," Abey explained, "and God instructed us to come to you. We've brought rugs and spices."

The king ordered that a feast be cooked, duck and rice and cucumber salad, za'atar flatbread and wine in goblets, chocolate baklava. A great staff of servants brought gleaming plates and took them away. The men talked about cures for famine and international politics while Sari sat in silence trying to eat her duck and rice daintily even though she was ravenous after many days of desert travel. Abey watched the way that the king and his son looked at Sari during the meal, as though it was her they'd rather be eating.

"It was brilliant that you introduced me as your sister," Sari whispered later, in the hallway outside their adjacent sleeping chambers.

"Brilliant?" Abey asked.

"Well, I am very beautiful," Sari explained, batting her eyes campily, realizing that Abey was pure-hearted and not so crafty and probably did not plan this out after all, "and now that I'm single, they'll almost definitely want my hand in marriage for one of the king's sons. They'll give us gifts to convince Daddy and we'll survive the drought."

"This is why God sent us here!" Abey realized. While many people believed in a God who cared about all his babies equally, Abey knew that he was Chosen, Special, like a true son to God. God had chosen him to father many nations, after all, and would have no problem tricking some less important king out of some animals and grain in order to get those nations birthed.

Indeed, the next morning the king asked Abey whether he would give Sari to be married to his son. "I'm honored," Abey said. "But it isn't for me to give that permission. Send us with gifts to present to our father. He is searching for a husband for Sari, and he's very picky. But I know my daddy. He'll be convinced by gifts that show him Sari will have a healthy, prosperous life. Send us back with gifts that assure him of this, and he'll say yes."

"Go right away then," said the king, "so that we might get an answer soon."

The king ordered servants to load Abey and Sari's wagon with foods that might carry them through their drought: dried figs and apricots, sacks of rice, wheels of cheese, pomegranates, two lambs for slaughter, two baby goats for milk. The king gifted an extra camel, too, to pull the now quite heavy wagon.

When the wagon was loaded, the king's son emerged from his chambers with a girl, barely teenaged, whom he directed by the shoulders. The girl walked shyly, doe-eyed and long-lashed and dark. "This is Hagar," the king's son said. "She is the daughter of my mother's handmaiden. I'd like to gift her to Sari."

Hagar knelt to the stone floor, bowed her head, and kissed Sari's feet.

"Oh, honey," Sari said. "That kind of subservience isn't necessary. We're very casual people. Come on, stand up." Sari reached for Hagar's hands and pulled her to her feet. "Thank you so much," Sari said to the king's son, putting her arms around Hagar. "I've never had my own girl before."

*   *   *

On the road back, Sari resumed her position with her legs behind Abey and Hagar sat in back with the baby animals.

"What will we tell the king?" Sari asked.

"We'll just tell him Dad found a boy for you back home while we were gone and we're so sorry," Abey shrugged.

Watching Hagar climb down from the wagon in front of the stone house, Sari felt newly struck by how young Hagar was, this child who'd been sent so far away from everything she knew. "Come on, baby doll, you've had a long journey. Why doesn't everyone have some supper and then we'll have someone show you the servant's quarters."

Hagar's presence rejuvenated Sari. Sari showed Hagar how to slice and grill cactus, she went walking with Hagar and collected dates and figs. Sari taught Hagar to accentuate her eyes with kohl and showed her how nice it is to spin under flowering trees in springtime. They spun side by side in the blue blue sky. Hagar bathed Sari in a large metal tub, pouring cups of water onto Sari's neck and shoulders, rubbing soap under Sari's arms. Hagar braided Sari's curly hair and rubbed floral creams into Sari's skin. Neither Hagar nor Sari could read, but they made up stories about girls and frogs and princes and witches and scary cats and told them to one another again and again, promising to remember the details the other forgot, filling in gaps for each other until eventually it was unclear who'd invented the story and who'd filled in the gaps.

On walks, they invented names for all the unnamed flowers. *Flipsissirilla, cupthula, wisteria, pudus.*

In the tub, Hagar soaped Sari's back and rubbed the dead skin off her heels with stones. One day Sari asked Hagar to get in the tub with her and on that day, she first saw what was between Hagar's legs, saw what looked like two nestled slugs.

When Sari couldn't sleep, she called Hagar in to hold her: it wouldn't have been appropriate to enter her husband's room to rouse him just for this; Abey had such important work to do, but this was Hagar's whole job, she justified. Hagar spooned Sari from behind and rubbed her shoulders and whispered sweet words like "You are drifting off on a puff of cloud shaped just like a dragon, Mistress, and your hair is made of long feathers" until Sari slept and Sari knew that this was what she wanted a girl for, all of this.

As the years passed, Abey grew despondent. "I'm supposed to father many nations," he sighed, as if in a daze.

"There, there, sweetheart," Sari said. She was experiencing a new youth with Hagar, baking experimental fruit pies and drinking tea under the moon. She wasn't thinking much about future nations.

Still, Sari was sad about her marriage. She wished Abey would just explode at her, some outpouring of emotion that at least meant they were connecting, but instead he greeted her distantly, absorbed in his work. Abey began to retire to his room at the end of the day to take his supper alone. Sari visited Abey's room once weekly, on Sabbath eve, for rote, baby-focused sex, sex during which Abey pumped mechanically and kept his eyes on the wall.

Sex grew worse and worse as the years and the trying went on. Abey used to rub and suck Sari's baby squash until it spurted in overwhelming delight, used to bite her nipples and caress her butt at generous length, but lately Abey only paid attention to Sari's hole, to the part that seemed necessary for child production. And since Sari was not producing any children, she found this extremely un-hot.

Eventually, the magic of having a girl around wore off a little, too.

"I'm bored," Sari said.

"I'm bored, too," Hagar confessed.

"I wish we had a baby," Sari said. She hadn't meant to say "we," but once it was out of her mouth, new things became possible. She looked at Hagar's face and saw a glimmer, Hagar's recognition of the possibilities, too.

"Yes," Hagar said, "I wish for that, too, Mistress."

"We'll have to convince Abey it's his idea," Sari said.

The next Sabbath eve, Sari visited Abey's chamber.

"Do you think it's hopeless?" Sari asked, after Abey finished. "We've been trying this for so many years."

"We have to keep trying," Abey said, but his eyes were just squints with eye-sized bags underneath and he sounded defeated. "You know we do, Sari."

"Ugh," Sari exclaimed, tossing her fists down at her sides. "I just feel like it's all my fault, like my body's wrong. Like, I've seen what Hagar has and you know what it looks like down there? It's two fat little slugs, nestling together, and I just feel like those slugs are nestling to protect a hole, the hole that goes up to where the baby lives, and maybe I just don't have that hole."

"Of course you do, babe," Abey said, rubbing Sari between

her shoulders. "It's right here," he said, tenderly pushing her little pink star.

Sari began to cry and cry, real tears. It wasn't until she described Hagar's slugs out loud that she knew for sure she did not have what it took to make a baby. Abey held her while she cried for her inadequacy, for her own stupidity all these years, for ruining Abey's destiny, for her dissolved marriage, etc. until she fell asleep in Abey's bed.

The next day, Abey requested to have dinner with Sari. It had been a long time. Lamb and rice tabbouleh were prepared, red wine poured.

"So, I talked to God," Abey said.

Sari raised her eyebrows expectantly.

"He wants that I should ask you something." He looked deeply into Sari's eyes and touched her hand. "Would you lend me Hagar? To carry our child, I mean?"

Sari feigned surprise. She set down her wineglass. "Wow," she said. "I have to think about it. It would be hard," she said, realizing it was true.

"She'll just be an external baby cooker," said Abey. "For *our* baby."

"Right," Sari said.

"Honey, look," Abey said, rubbing her hand. "Hagar is our property. We can put her to use in whatever way best serves us. Plus, it's what God suggests."

"It's a suggestion that makes a lot of sense," Sari said. "Baruch ha shem," she added, feeling like maybe it sounded disrespectful for her to determine whether God's suggestions made sense or not.

"Spend a night and think about it," said Abey. "It's your decision."

Sari slept alone that night. This was her idea that she'd planted into Abey's brain and now she kind of hated it. The next morning, Sari was sitting at her vanity, pinning her curls up in scorpion-shell combs and thinking when Hagar came in with fresh sheets. "Abey's agreed to the plan," Sari said coolly, eyeing Hagar in the mirror's reflection for part of a second. "You'll come with me next Shabbas to Abey's room and he'll try to put our baby in you." The "our" was vague and Sari liked it that way. It left open that Hagar might be included in the baby's parentage or she might not.

Hagar clutched the sheets she was holding, stopped still. "That wasn't the plan," she said slowly.

Sari kept gazing at Hagar in the mirror as she coiled a chunk of hair around her finger and pinned it back. "We didn't make a plan," Sari said. "Anyway, plans are not ours to make."

"The plan..." Hagar started. "Never mind." Hagar could see that Sari seemed distant and vexed. She lowered her head and made a hospital corner.

Hagar's plan, which she *thought* Sari understood via their psychic connection and subtle communication, came from Mother Nature. Mother Nature, herself a fat, furry, and oozing dyke, was sick of God always having the upper hand. "I'm not a fan of that God," Mother Nature told Hagar. "He's always trying to shrink things to fit his ego. The earth is magnificent, fruit everywhere, flowing water, continuous joyous eating and fucking on every level of existence, a never-ending cacophonous gorgeous throbbing of attraction and pursuit and swallowing and merging and birthing but that God, he wants everything contained and organized," Mother Nature said. "He will kill me eventually, run the waterfalls dry and sterilize the soil and kill all the tiny creatures that make the fruits grow, kill all the mushrooms small and great that enable plants to talk to one another and to the creatures who eat them. If it were up to God, no one would get any messages from the plants, and voila, I'm dead." Mother Nature wanted Hagar and Sari to make the baby, she said, and to leave Abey out of it. "I am not in favor of nations," Mother Nature told Hagar. "Lesbians should be the mothers of the future humans of this earth. And you and Sari will be able to make a baby."

Once Sari agreed to lend Hagar, Abey warmed to her again. With Abey's affection, Sari began to look at things differently. *I love Hagar and I love Abey*, Sari thought. *Maybe it would be nice to see them love each other.*

We know the sex scene with Abey, Sari, and Hagar was sterilized in that book that's in every hotel nightstand drawer and then copied to very creepy effect in *The Handmaid's Tale*, but look: Sari was not standing behind Hagar chastely holding her hands. We're not going to describe it all here, but we can tell you that it started with Hagar in cat pose with Abey behind her and Hagar and Sari face-to-face, and ended with all three passed out in a haphazard pile with limbs everywhere extending to all corners of the bed.

From then on, they all dined together, Hagar at Sari's side and Abey across the table.

"Hagar is like an extension of you now, babe," Abey said. "She's your womb."

This statement grossed out both Sari and Hagar who, for different reasons, were invested in seeing Hagar as a separate person.

After dinner, Hagar followed Sari into her room to unpin her hair.

"Do you think you're pregnant, darling?" Sari asked as chunks of curls shook loose from their pins.

"Of course not," Hagar responded. "A child can only take root when the moon is new, when it's dark, I mean, or the tiniest sliver of a crescent." She unclasped a hairpin. "Our activity took place under a half moon."

"If you knew your body wouldn't conceive under the half moon," Sari said, clearly irritated, "why would you have us engage in such *activity* at all?"

"Did you not have fun?" Hagar asked, a corner of her lip turning into a smile, which Sari could see in the mirror in front of her.

Sari sighed. "It complicates the dynamic."

"Or it could simplify the dynamic," Hagar said, beginning to brush Sari's hair. "Mistress?" Hagar said. "I have a plan, is the thing. I would like to tell you, but I hope you won't be angry."

"I'm sort of angry already, honey," Sari said.

"I thought you and I could do it," Hagar said quickly, with childish enthusiasm she couldn't contain. "I thought we could make the many nations together. I think we can."

Sari felt stunned. She hadn't considered that the two of them could make a baby. But she liked the idea of no longer being left out of the very Special baby-making. "It's not what God wants," Sari said.

"Well, Abey would never have to know," Hagar tried nervously.

Sari chewed on a hairpin and thought about this. "It's a good idea," she said. "Please be in charge of making it happen."

When the moon was empty, Hagar laid Sari out on the bed like a beautiful virgin, in a cream silk robe and squatted over Sari's center. The slugs at Hagar's own center parted in order to suck on the little pink summer squash between Sari's thighs and the muscular cavern Hagar's slugs protected swallowed and Sari moaned and Hagar bounced her hips and shouted as if possessed. Sari screamed out and Hagar extracted out the seawaterish potion that she knew was there, that she knew could make a baby under the dark moon.

During the pregnancy, Sari rubbed Hagar's feet and ordered her special teas. She invited Hagar to sleep beside her, so she could hold her around her center and whisper to their baby, so she could feel its first kick.

"The two of you truly are as one flesh," Abey remarked biblically, seeing Hagar and Sari huddled together over Hagar's eight-month belly.

"Ew," Sari whispered when he walked away. Both women giggled.

When Ishmael was born, Abey said that he looked just like Sari. He was trying to be kind, only, but it was true. Ishmael had Sari's loose curls and clear cattish eyes, Hagar's straighter nose and plumper lips. Sari and Hagar each felt a deep sense of connection to and even ownership of the baby. Of course, Abey did, too.

"God is so happy you've finally given birth to my baby that he would like to change your name," Abey said to Sari. "Because of your great sacrifice, God wants to give you a more womanly name," Abey said. "He'd like to rename you Sarah."

Mother Nature was thrilled upon Ishmael's birth. She believed that lesbian mothers would thwart the building of nations, that from here on out, humanity would be gawping up at tree limbs, slicing and grilling cacti, cumming all over each other in the sand, eating the magical mushrooms she'd strewn around for them so that they could talk to the plants. Mother Nature's waterfalls surged foamily in celebration; her mud pits burbled wetly; her cicadas cast off their shells and sang; the tiniest soil creatures stirred with desire to merge and swallow and birth, a volcano somewhere erupted in joy.

For the first couple of years, more fruit grew, more rains came and Hagar and Sarah were happy. Each felt the dissolution that comes with new motherhood. They felt blurred at the edges, with the baby, the fruit, the sand, each other. Sarah got Hagar her own maid so that both women could lounge, make up stories and tell them to the baby, cuddle, present Ishy with different fruits and desert flowers, watch and laugh as he smashed the fragrant colors into his face. Hagar breastfed and Sarah rocked the baby to sleep. They all three spooned.

Abey loved to see the bond between the baby and his mom and his nursemaid. He and Sarah were on a post-baby sex break. Sometimes Sarah and Hagar would plot out how to get Abey to come over and sexually service each of them, but instead they'd end up laughing and then kissing and cuddling and sometimes lazily rubbing each other to orgasm while Ishy slept in his cradle.

But after Ishmael began to talk, Abey invited Sarah to a serious dinner. Sarah got out of her floral robe and into a fitted dress, and joined Abey for duck and tubers and wine.

"It's been so wonderful that Hagar has been able to be so present in the baby's life," Abey said.

"It totally has," Sarah said.

"And that you've been so comfortable with her and Ishmael's connection," he added.

"I have," Sarah said, nervously swooshing her wine in the glass.

"Really, it's beautiful to watch," Abey said, serving Sarah some duck from a large platter. "But now that the child is weaned, I think it's time for Hagar to return to the servant's quarters, and for Ishmael to get his own room."

Sarah didn't want things to change, but what could she say? She had known, throughout the idyll of Ishy's infancy, that this couldn't last forever, this mushy time of flower-smelling and afternoon naps, this blur of day and night. She hadn't thought about it a lot, but she had known.

"I've gotten Ishmael a tutor," Abey said. "He'll begin his training next week."

Sarah balked at the word "training." Like a dancing bear, she thought. "I'm sad to realize he's growing up so fast," Sarah admitted. "But you're right, he has to be schooled."

"Sar?" Abey asked, placing a hand on Sarah's shoulder. "Please see that Hagar's time with Ishmael is limited. I love that you've all been close during Ishmael's babyhood, and it made sense, since Hagar was nursing, but a growing boy really shouldn't be too attached to his nursemaid."

Sarah squirmed away from Abey's hand and glowered at her duck. "I wish I had known you felt this way before Hagar and Ishy were practically inseparable," she said.

"Babies are taken from maids all the time," Abey said. "Both acclimate. Ishmael needs to be clear that you are his mother. Don't you want that?" He parked his fork in the duck and used his knife to lob off a piece. "You don't want Ishy to be confused."

Confusion didn't seem like the worst imaginable thing to Sarah who, herself, felt confused. But then she understood that this was the way things happened. Ishmael was supposed to be the beginning of the nations Abey was supposed to father, and nation-founders probably weren't flower-sniffing daytime snugglers.

"Okay," Sarah agreed, "I'll move Hagar out."

Sarah spoke coldly when she announced the news to Hagar. It would have been too painful to do it any other way. "We have to get real, honey," she said. "Ishy's going to be a prince or whatever, and we have to let Abey get him groomed for that. I mean, that was the whole point of all of this."

"God's nations," Hagar said. She didn't really have an argument to make in response, at least not one she thought would be well-received.

Hagar packed a bag and walked the one hundred and seven steps from Sarah and Ishmael's room to her own long-abandoned hut calmly, closed the door behind her, and then collapsed on her lumpy mattress thrown in the corner of the cold stone floor and wept.

But soon they settled into a new routine: Ishmael was tutored during the day, supped with Sarah, and was put to bed by Hagar just before Sarah was put to bed by Hagar.

"Shouldn't you put Ishmael to bed?" Abey asked Sarah.

"I'm tired," Sarah said, but the truth was she felt giving Hagar a little bit of daily solo time with Ishy—a chance to tell him her stories and kiss his face—was the least she could do.

All three learned the feeling of sleeping alone. Sleeping alone, all three dreamed more vividly, but no one was there to hold them tight when they made little nightmare sounds. Occasionally, Ishmael would run down the hall to Sarah's room and climb into bed with her. Sarah feigned irritation but was happy to have Ishmael's little limbs clutching her, happy to run her fingers through his soft baby hair until they both fell asleep again. Occasionally, too, Sarah would creep out the door, careful not to let it creak, and walk the one hundred and seven steps through the sand to Hagar's hut where Hagar pretended to acquiesce to Sarah's needy caresses, but was mostly thrilled to receive her. On these nights, they rubbed against each other like they were starving, inserting fingers and tongues everywhere. And then Sarah was gone.

One night, when Ishmael was five, Sarah and Abey hosted a feast to show off their tiny future leader. All kinds of Special people from neighboring clans attended. Hagar served at the feast, carrying platters of various kinds of fowl, sliced figs, rice, and green vegetables. She couldn't help thinking about planting those vegetables side by side with Sarah, with the baby on her hip, about letting Ishy pick figs and smush them into his mouth.

Because she was perceived as background, Hagar heard people whisper about how dark the young child was, darker than both Sarah and Abey, and this pleased her, but everyone also commented on how poised Ishy was, how serious and quiet. Ishmael looked so natural in formalwear, they all said, you could see that he was indeed going to be a leader.

For her part, Sarah found great pleasure in dressing up in gowns, in having Hagar pin her hair up glamorously like old times. She loved being pulled in a wagon by camel for the several acres to the tent that had been set up for the occasion and feeling Ishmael's little body fall asleep against her during the ride. She loved being admired by so many strangers, being called beautiful, being told her child was beautiful.

Hagar went back to her hut early—there were lesser servants to pour late-night wine, to clean up the mess.

Sarah appeared, drunk and far past midnight, at Hagar's bedside. Hagar invited her to lie down. She held Sarah and stroked her hair and then said plainly, "Sari, I'm going to leave." (She had never gotten used to calling Sarah by the name God chose.)

Sarah's first response was to laugh, as though Hagar was playing a fantasy game. "Where will you go?" she asked.

"I'm not sure," Hagar answered. "But I hate this. I want to be a mother to our child. I want our child to call me mother and I want to be presented as his mother and I want to choose how he is raised. I don't even know who Ishmael is now—he's like a dancing bear, all the wildness trained out of him. And I've just been forgotten. Now that he eats food that doesn't come from my body, I have no purpose here."

Sarah recoiled a little despite herself. It's easy to feel disgust with desperation when you have mostly everything you want.

"I haven't forgotten you," Sarah said.

"That's great," said Hagar. "Because I want you and Ishmael to come. We can go where we can be a family."

"Where do you propose we go?" Sarah asked, sounding more amused than she would have liked.

"We'll take the carriage and go until we find somewhere we can live. We'll take animals and skeins of water and seeds and a tent. People have been doing this for all of time."

"We can't," Sarah said.

"Why not?" Hagar asked.

The truth was Sarah had grown accustomed to luxury. She still enjoyed desert strolls and short journeys, but she loved her bed, her silk dressing gown, her floral creams, her vanity, her chickens. She relied on having servants to cook her goose when she wanted.

"I can't," Sarah clarified.

"Oh," Hagar said. "I see."

"I'll help you get back to Egypt if that would suit you better. You've served me well and I would miss you awfully, but I want you to be happy."

"I hadn't thought about that," said Hagar, "but I guess Ishmael and I could go to Egypt."

"Ishmael?" Sarah said. "You literally cannot. Ishmael is mine and Abey's according to law. You know that, honey."

*　　*　　*

And this is how Hagar came to kidnap her own baby in the middle of the night and wander out into the desert, disappearing for years. She was not about to make decisions based on notions of people as property according to law. She followed the laws of Mother Nature, which were governance only by hunger and love. Hagar felt she was not abandoning Sarah, but that Sarah had abandoned her, had become someone totally unknown to her, someone who failed to recognize who she was, who they had been together, who they and their child could be. It was easier than she thought it would be, to enter the house quietly, to pack up food and water, to rouse Ishy, to take his hand and leave.

Sarah sunk into a loneliness like she'd never known. The trees no longer brought her joy and nothing else did either, not sex nor affection nor roasted goose. She was so old. Publicly, out of simple exhaustion, she endorsed the gossip about her evil maid who stole her only child and fled, nodding along and making noises of lazy assent to whomever was speaking. Privately, she ate very little, braided and unbraided her hair, began to visit Abey's room on Shabbas again for sweet and lazy or rote and disconnected love, depending on her mood.

You know the rest of the story: God decided Sarah had proved her loyalty to him and somehow therefore proved her femininity, too, and so he finally did the miracle Sarah had wanted so long ago, but which she had given up thinking about entirely. Sarah became pregnant. She named the baby Isaac so that she could call him Izzy, which was close to Ishy.

Hagar and Ishmael, meanwhile, camped, foraged, and made fires at night to stay warm. Hagar told Ishmael stories she'd grown up on and stories she'd invented with Sarah. They developed skills by eating plants and mushrooms and listening to the voice of Mother Nature, and they collected rainwater to drink.

One day, the rainwater ran out. Hagar and Ishmael grew sick and weak. Hagar began to see visions of the angel of death. She did not want to die, but more than that, she did not want Ishmael to die. She called upon Mother Nature. *I do not do miracles,* Mother Nature shrugged. *But lucky for you, there is a spring a little ways up. Walk directly toward the sun and soon you'll get to drink.*

Hagar walked and walked toward the sun with Ishy, now a tall child of uncountable wild years, beside her. Eventually she collapsed in a bawling heap, unable to go further, sure they would both die. It was God who spoke to her then.

"Congratulations, Hagar," God said, in the voice of a game show host. "You have made it to the spring. However, I have hidden the spring from you."

Hagar wanted to scream that God was a fucking prick but instead she asked, "Oh God, whatever can I do for you to make the spring reappear?"

"If you agree to return to Abey's house, so that Ishmael can fulfill his destiny of fathering a great nation, I will unhide the spring."

Forced between allowing her child to father nations and allowing her child to die, Hagar agreed. There was time, she reasoned, to get out of nation-fathering later. So God unhid the spring and they drank and Hagar returned to the stone house in terror for her child.

Sarah's heart leapt at seeing Hagar, but she acted reserved. She couldn't risk being abandoned again—her pain was too great. The two never shared a bed again, except very close to the time of Sarah's death.

Izzy and Ishy lived under the same roof as brothers. Izzy was studious and prissy and well-kept; Ishy had regained his wildness in the desert and was outdoorsy and muscular and could talk to plants. Sarah spent her attention on Izzy but watched Ishy longingly, with love and pride—he seemed truly like her and Hagar's child. Their love still mingled in him and seeing it there made Sarah's heart swell.

Ishy resented Izzy's prissiness and mocked him for it. Izzy resented Ishy's strength and wisdom and tried always to engage him in the sorts of competitions he was certain to win. Privately, Ishy studied, and he learned quickly and began to surpass Izzy. Privately, Izzy went out to the desert to try to regain his wildness—he would feel Mother Nature's power for a moment, witnessing a yellow flower emerge from the top of a cactus or a leaping baby jackrabbit with ears shaped like the succulents around him, but ultimately, Izzy was too close to God. In some ways, it was an average sort of sibling rivalry, but the nations they birthed are still warring. "That's how it is with nations," we can hear Mother Nature croak from her deathbed. "Nations war." God has of course vanquished Mother Nature; many of her rivers are trickles and most of her plants are mute, but sometimes we find the ones that aren't, and then, in the creakiest and most staticky of voices, we can hear her.

She told us this story after we ate some foraged mushrooms in aquafaba cream sauce over orecchiette but she cut out every two seconds and we had to fill in the gaps and in the end we're not sure if we've transcribed it faithfully, or if we've made it all up.

GEMSTONES

Ry kept announcing that they were taking the day off—what from, it wasn't clear. Most days, Ry stretched out on the couch in their gray sweatshirt dress clicking around the internet and called it working. Ry would do some freelance editing and social media updates for some jobs, and then spend the rest of the day positioned to start writing a poem at any time. Ry knew this would be more likely to happen if they took a walk or went to the zoo or something but some combination of guilt, exhaustion, fake work ethic, and body image issues kept them stuck on the couch in a garment stained with what looked like toothpaste, olive oil, ink. How do you take a day off, Ry wondered, from what might look, to an external observer, like a day off already?

Manny went to actual work in clean, fitted clothes, expensive shoes and glasses, then came home, put a bunch of tortilla chips in a bowl, squeezed lemon and Tapatío all over them, and started drinking beers. Ry would still be there on the couch, clicking. Ry didn't drink until midnight, when Manny was asleep—until then, Ry thought, they might start working.

"There needs to be some kind of boundary between your work and your life," Manny said.

"I'm a poet," said Ry, clicking a pleather baseball cap into their online shopping cart.

In day-off stories, there were always parents to escape from. Ferris Bueller had parents. Bill and Ted had parents. Even Dorothy had parental figures. Ry didn't have any parents, but Ry had Manny.

It's not that Ry's relationship with Manny was bad; it was just that sometimes it was hard to tell if it was good. In the media Ry consumed, the lesbians died, or else they were a fierce cadre with a radical mission, or they were tragic and obsessed and etching hearts into each other's thighs. Lesbians weren't supposed to be tragic anymore, at least not more so than anyone else, and Manny was a picky graphic designer who would only let someone etch something into their skin if they were, like, a professional charging money, plus, Ry was too inertia-sucked to figure out how to find a radical mission, and so it was sometimes hard to know if they were doing their lesbian relationship well, to locate, among all the moments of reinvention and assimilation, the markers of success and failure.

While Ry was wrapped in towels post-shower, Manny came into the bathroom.

"What's that theorist guy you like say?" Manny asked. "Queerness is not yet here?" Manny was trying to connect to Ry on Ry's terms.

"Yeah, queerness is not yet here," Ry repeated. "José Muñoz."

"Well it's not yet here," Manny declared. "So for now, you gotta figure out how to get that period stain out of the sheets before it's bedtime, or else go to Target to get some new ones."

Manny was always trying to make Ry go to Target, alone during the week or together on Saturdays. Ry never went alone, which annoyed Manny, who saw Ry as having endless time. But while Manny's time was partitioned out into different kinds of productive and life-improving tasks, Ry's time stretched and blurred, disappearing in a way they couldn't account for. Ry hated being at Target on a Saturday; they wanted to be full of passion and still in bed or full of passion at a demonstration at City Hall. But Manny would insist they needed a storage solution for the overflowing pills and skin-care products in the bathroom—all Ry's—and anyway, Manny swore, their brown gender-nonconforming presence somewhere fancy grabbing a post-Target mimosa had more political import than if they were just another body in a sweaty sea of protesters.

Jamie, the impetus for Ry's day off, had arrived in Ry's city two nights before. Even though Ry had met Jamie only once before, they'd gone to pick Jamie up from the airport. Ry found it easy to be nice to people before getting to know them well enough to find them disappointing, and Ry liked Jamie; they'd met at a poetry conference two years ago, just after the release of Ry's first and only book of poems, when Jamie had approached Ry, gushy, and told them Ry's book was their favorite of the year. "Oh my god, are we going to be best friends?" Ry had asked.

*   *   *

They hadn't become best friends, but the poetry conference was in Ry's city this time, and somehow things turned out so that Jamie was staying at Ry's house. Manny hated this quality of Ry's, their tendency to just end up with houseguests. Ry saw no need to prepare for these guests, while Manny needed the toilet bowl and sinks to be shining and every cabinet interior to be perfectly organized.

After the first day of the conference, Ry and Jamie sat on the couch, Ry in overalls and a crop top and Jamie in tight Bermuda shorts and a black mesh T-shirt, and drank Prosecco, discussing which talks were good and which were boring and who had cool outfits. Manny sat on the other end of the couch drinking a beer and looking at their phone.

"I liked Matt's stuff about the eternal adolescence of queer voices," said Ry.

"Me too!" Jamie said. "I feel eternally adolescent! It's sad, though, Matt's been considering stopping writing. He says the world doesn't need any more white gay poets."

"That's so cool," Manny said. "Like...is he also going to kill himself?" Manny got up and headed toward the kitchen.

Jamie laughed uncomfortably. "Oh my god, Manny's so intense," said Jamie, once Manny had disappeared.

On the second day of the conference, Ry and Jamie took the day off. While Manny was making coffee, Ry approached from behind, leaning into Manny's back and asking if Manny wanted to take the day off, too, but Manny insisted Ry and Jamie had their own special poet bond, that they should spend some time alone together.

"You know, you and Jamie should go talk about, like, the relationship status and outfit of every poet you both know in peace," Manny said.

"Please?" said Ry.

"You and Jamie are kind of annoying me, babe," Manny said, wrapping up Ry's body in a hug. "Plus, I have to go to work."

"You could have just said the work part," said Ry.

"Come on. Go have a good day, Rhizome." Manny rubbed Ry vigorously between the shoulders.

Ry looked up at Manny. "Okay, okay. You too, Manuela."

"Can we get dinner later, though?" Manny asked.

"K," said Ry.

Ry and Jamie boarded a train that ran along the concrete basin of a former river to a miniature, imagined version of a Japanese city. Neither Ry nor Jamie had been to the real Japan, but in this miniature version, everything was cute. The stores sold makeup palettes and pastel puffballs you could wear in your hair, candy-colored desserts and Hello Kitty toasters. There were plush animals of all kinds—big-eyed, chubby, pastel hamsters and hot-pink snow leopards and little dogs with their imaginary hairs cut into perfect squares like Japanese pets Ry and Jamie had seen on the internet. There were French-fry earrings.

They wandered into a velvet-painting museum run by an old punk in high-waisted jeans and a moppy mustache that looked adhesived onto his face. He told them about his collection of velvet paintings, the largest in the world, and lamented the increasing rents all over the city. "You might be some of the last visitors," he said. It made them both sad. There were velvet paintings of a topless and seductive Anderson Cooper, a fur-covered Liberace whose jewels glinted in the light like they were real, a cornucopia of Virgin Marys and Elvises. They sat on zebra-striped beanbag chairs and smoked mint-flavored weed out of a vape pen.

When Ry and Jamie emerged from the museum, they saw a store that looked like a cosmetics counter but whose sign displayed a row of glowing, empty macarons that looked like fat and gleaming labia majora. "I love macarons," Jamie said. They went inside and got a bag and then sat on a concrete step, eating them: lemon, raspberry, pistachio, lavender. Jamie took a bite of each macaron and then passed it to Ry.

Jamie told Ry about a cartoon show they loved where the characters were modeled after gemstones. Sometimes the gemstones would fuse, so that Ruby and Sapphire became a whole new gemstone, many times the size of either Ruby or Sapphire alone. The new gemstone possessed entirely new superpowers, like hyper speed or a future-seeing third eye. Did Jamie think the two of them could merge and develop superpowers? Ry didn't normally smoke a lot of weed and they were, they were realizing, stoned. Ry shoved a half-eaten hot pink macaron in their mouth.

"This is one of the only neighborhoods made for femmes," Jamie said.

Ry's mouth felt full of crackly sugar, of *pinkness*. The macaron was buying them time to respond but they felt like they couldn't figure out what a macaron *was* and that felt unsettling. Was it a cookie? A candy? Cake? "Most of the world is so not cute," said Ry finally. "There's this one cute store here with a pink dumpster and I think a lot about, like, what if all dumpsters were pink?"

"Pink dumpsters would be amazing," said Jamie. "I mean who is even designing the world?"

"Manny," said Ry.

"Manny's cool though," Jamie said.

"I guess," said Ry. "It's just...I don't know. Relationships are hard."

"For me, too," Jamie said. "Which makes sense because I think we're basically the same person."

"I was just reading this essay," said Ry, "about how fags and hags together are able to resist the pull of homonormativity and enter a kind of ecstatic queer time, in a way that's impossible within a couple formation."

"Ew," Jamie said. "That's so binary, Ry."

"Okay, sorry," said Ry, worried they had ruined everything. "Language is also hard."

"Not really," Jamie said. "Let's go into the mall."

In the mall Ry and Jamie wandered into, most of the stores were closed, and they seemed to be the only ones there. They were flanked by empty photo booths and shop windows displaying plush, neon snow leopards and tiny dresses emblazoned with photorealistic palm trees. "I feel like I've already had a dream about this," Jamie said.

Jamie got caught up trying to win a bunny from one of those machines with a crane that descends on a pit of toys. Ry watched as the crane swallowed the bunny's head, lightly grazed up the length of the bunny's ears, and then snapped its jaws in the air above them. "This machine is a scam," Ry said. "The laws of physics will never allow you to get that bunny."

* * *

Ry wandered farther down the mall. In a dusty and neglected corner was what looked like a photo booth with purple curtains and a sign in silver caps that spelled out THE SARAH MACHINE.

Ry felt called and even though they only had forty-six dollars left in their bank account, Ry swiped their credit card to pay the sixteen dollars the machine requested. ONE PLAYER OR TWO? the machine's touch screen prompted. Ry touched ONE. SELECT YOUR SARAH, the touch screen said. This was a difficult choice. Ry watched the names of all the Sarahs flashing in pixilated caps on the screen. TIME IS RUNNING OUT!!! the touchscreen warned, flashing a timer graphic. "Fine," Ry said. They selected SARAH PAULSON. Sarah Paulson was so stunning, such a glamorous and truly grown-up lesbian. Ry saw their own face and body appear on the screen and watched as a bouncing oval encircled it. Ry heard a scissory clipping sound, after which Ry's face remained onscreen, but their hair was replaced with slicked-back platinum hair. The screen split in two and Sarah Paulson's face appeared on the other half of the screen. Sarah Paulson's eyes instructed Ry on how to gaze: straight forward, intense, more intense, no not quite that intense, Ry mimicked, adjusted. Ry as Sarah Paulson was totally self-contained, they weren't going to merge with anyone to become a super gemstone or whatever. Ry had strong brows now, onscreen. Ry's own brows were normally sparse and disconnected and these sparse brows contributed significantly, Ry felt, to the dumb receptive quality of Ry's face. On the screen in front of Ry, Ry's face was Ry's face, but it was trained into doing something Ry's face could not normally do; into doing something only Sarah Paulson's face could do. The camera snapped. The screen turned gray. A series of outfits appeared in rows of thumbnails. Ry picked a red plasticky dress with pouf princess sleeves. Their lips turned red and their skin dewy. Ry marveled at how, as Sarah Paulson, they could look so self-contained in plasticky princess sleeves. It was something about the gaze—how it contained no anger but also no invitation. The hair helped, too, the height and solidity of it. Sarah Paulson was here for her own good time. Ry marveled to think that Sarah Paulson had used her abundant sexual currency for her job only, and then chosen to love a woman over seventy, a person in the category of people with the least sexual currency of all. Ry imagined flouncing home in this red plastic dress to greet Holland Taylor. It made Ry smile—a joyful, unsolicitous smile. The camera snapped.

Jamie wandered over while Ry waited. "You were right about the bunny," Jamie said.

"I know," said Ry. It felt good to have Jamie say they were right about something, even if it was something un-important.

Then Jamie looked over the machine. "Did you do this?" Jamie asked.

Ry nodded. "It's powerful," Ry said.

"I want to do it," said Jamie, swiping their card.

ONE PLAYER OR TWO? the machine prompted. Jamie chose TWO. The screen prompted Player One to select a Sarah. "This is so hard," Jamie said, as the names of the Sarahs scrolled by. Jamie whined softly as each name disappeared.

"Oh my god, Sarah Schulman!" Jamie shouted, and pressed

a rectangle. It became Ry's turn to select a Sarah. They selected SARAH SILVERMAN.

KARAOKE OR IMPROMPTU? prompted the touch screen.

"Karaoke?" said Ry, and Jamie touched the karaoke rectangle.

The screen split into quadrants: Jamie and Sarah Schulman, Ry and Sarah Silverman. Then each pair merged.

"This is so weird," said Jamie.

"So weird," repeated Sarah Schulman's voice.

"So weird," repeated Jamie, their own voice adjusting to match.

"Weird," said Sarah Schulman.

"Weird," said Jamie.

The machine dinged.

"I love you as Sarah Schulman!" said Ry. Sarah Silverman's voice corrected Ry until she was repeating, "I love you as Sarah Schulman!" what felt like full octaves higher.

The machine dinged. A bouncing ball followed words on the screen, and Ry and Jamie read them.

"Hi, Sarah," Jamie said. Their voice sounded like Sarah Schulman's voice, or at least like what Ry imagined Sarah Schulman's voice would be like: sonorous, knowing, Jewish.

"Hi, Sarah," said Ry in Sarah Silverman's wise toddler voice.

There were bouncing balls like it was karaoke.

"Sarah, I want you to read my book as though you're watching a play," Jamie said.

"I love plays!" exclaimed Ry, nasal and charming. "But so, you don't want me to argue?"

"No, you can argue. I just want you to understand that, like in a play, some things will resonate, some will be rejected, and others might provoke you to produce new knowledge."

"You sound like my nana," Ry-as-Sarah-Silverman said. "That makes me feel so safe."

"That's nice, Sarah, but whether I sound like your nana or not shouldn't determine your level of safety. People are perceived as threats simply for being unfamiliar, and this misperception can lead to incarceration and death." Jamie's hands gesticulated on-screen, following Sarah Schulman's. It was like the hands were speaking their own, separate language. The camera snapped.

"Ughhhhh, you're so smart, Sarah," Ry-as-Sarah-Silverman said. "I really want to see your vagina. Your labia majora," they pronounced. "It sounds like a constellation but it's not, it's vagina lips."

"I want to say, Sarah," Jamie-as-Sarah-Schulman replied, "that while I'm uncomfortable, I don't see your desire as an attack. And I hope you don't see my rejection as an attack. Living with other people outside a supremacist structure involves being uncomfortable sometimes."

"Don't worry, Sarah," Ry-as-Sarah-Silverman said. "As a lifelong bed-wetter, I stopped feeling attacked by rejection long ago."

When the dialogue was over, the screen prompted, PICK OUT OUTFITS. Sarah Schulman came with a selection of button-ups, cardigans, and pullover sweaters. Sarah Silverman had a wardrobe of overalls, a horizontally striped turtleneck, a '70s Little League tee. Ry clicked liquid cat-eye liner on and off their hybridized face indecisively.

"Wow, I feel possessed," Ry said, still in Sarah Silverman's voice.

"It's really great to be possessed by Sarah Schulman," said Jamie. "Do you want to do it again?"

"It's sixteen dollars," Ry whined.

Jamie swiped their card. "I'm on vacation."

"Okay, but then can I have a turn being Sarah Schulman, too?" asked Ry.

"Do it," Jamie said. "It seems great to have Sarah Schulman as everyone's interlocutor."

Ry laughed and pressed the SCHULMAN rectangle.

"Oh my god, Sarah Edmondson!" said Jamie, pressing the button to select her. "Do you know her? The cult lady?"

"Yeah," said Ry. "This guy I went to camp with was in the very same cult."

KARAOKE OR IMPROMPTU? prompted the touch screen.

"Karaoke again, right?" Jamie said, pressing the rectangle.

Ry watched onscreen as their face aged, one cheek sagging slightly and eyes bagging a little. There was a strange comfort for Ry in seeing how they might look in thirty years. Clothes popped up first this time, inexplicably. A sleeveless button-up or a magenta cotton V-neck. Ry picked the V-neck. Ry as Sarah Schulman felt like a real queer intellectual, not someone with cool glasses and an expensive haircut they needed to constantly maintain, but someone who wasn't there to be looked at at all. As Sarah Schulman, Ry could see, they had abandoned the male gaze and maybe all gazes except the ones of those who wanted to look at their genius straight on, or those who wanted to co-create a new world. Ry smiled at their reflection. "I don't think I have ever felt attracted to Sarah Schulman, but I am oddly turned on by *being* Sarah Schulman," said Ry.

"*Being* Sarah Schulman," repeated Sarah Schulman's voice.

"*Being* Sarah Schulman," Ry repeated, trying to mimic the tone.

The machine dinged.

Jamie's cheekbones protruded out from their face then, and their hair grew long, black, flat-ironed. They were put into a basic tank and jeans, no options.

"I don't even get accessories?" Jamie said.

There wasn't, weirdly, any dinging for Sarah Edmondson's voice. It's like her voice could be any voice, like it didn't matter.

A bouncing ball followed words on the screen, and Ry and Jamie read them.

"How did I end up here?" Jamie said. They seemed frazzled, caught off-guard. "Who are you anyway?"

"Sarah Schulman," Ry said.

"Sarah Schulman," said Jamie. "Did I read you in college?" They squinted for a second, not long enough to wait for an answer. "That's good, you're smart. I need to talk to someone smart. Everyone keeps talking about how strong I am and maybe that's true. It's hard to leave a cult. But the truth is I feel like a mess. Their ideas were my ideas, their whole framework was my whole framework. It was like, I only knew how to see from inside that framework, and then one day, something happened and I could only see the framework from the outside. Has that ever happened to you, Sarah?"

"Well, Sarah," Ry said, "we're all inside structures of power all the time. We have to work to continue to see them, to know how they're shaping our perceptions."

"I keep thinking of this line," said Jamie, "from when I was on *My Little Pony: Friendship Is Magic*. I was a blue Pegasus with orange bangs and I was talking to this other pony, a tiny orange one, and I said, '*Scootaloo, you are just so great at blindfolds.*'"

Ry-as-Schulman laughed. "Cults are really great at blind-folds," they said. "But mostly people everywhere work hard to keep their blindfolds on. People work to avoid being alone because what people see when they're alone can drive them crazy."

"Yeah, the kind of secret thing," Jamie said, "is I *do* feel crazy. I hate being alone. My best friend Lauren had me branded like an animal but the fucked-up thing is sometimes I miss her so much I would put my blindfold back on if only I could figure out how."

"I get that, Sarah," said Ry. "I mean truly. Friendship *is* magic, as you say. And to me it makes sense that you'd have trouble finding real friendship while trying to be an artist in the era of gentrification. When I was in my twenties, we had cheap rent, and there was time to wander the neighborhood, to play around and make all kinds of theater, theater that was bad, even. We could do that and still have time to gather, to organize ways to shift the world, to change the state's relationship to us, the conditions of our lives." It felt good to declaim, Ry felt. "These days, a bowl of noodles costs fourteen bucks." Ry put a hand between Jamie's shoulders. "Noodles ease the path to the kind of conversations that invite the collective imagination necessary for both theater and radical organizing."

"I haven't eaten noodles in years," said Jamie-as-Edmondson.

Ry-as-Schulman looked at Jamie sadly. They were not surprised.

The session ended.

Ry thought about Manny, how Manny had to be the one who was a servant to capitalism all the time so that Ry could make bad art and try to engage or connect or whatever. "God, I feel like it takes literally becoming someone for me to learn anything," said Ry. "Do you think that's a learning disability?"

"Maybe," Jamie responded. "Can we do it just one more time? Like with some funner Sarahs?"

They chose SARAH JESSICA PARKER and SARAH MICHELLE GELLAR, IMPROMPTU.

"I've wanted to be SJP ever since *Girls Just Want to Have Fun*," Ry said, hair poofing out as they learned to smile a cute, disarming smile, "when she proved that even a goody-two-shoes daddy's girl could become cool, could become *a TV dancer*, if only her true secret passion was witnessed by an adventurous loner with taste."

"Oh my god, am I the adventurous loner?" Jamie asked as their hair grew shoulder-length, and their voice adjusted.

They looked together at their cute, blond lady looks.

"We're such different Jews now," said Ry-as-Sarah-Jessica-Parker.

"Blond Jews," Jamie-as-Sarah-Michelle-Gellar replied.

"Blond changes everything," Ry-as-SJP said. "I remember this line I said to you when I cameoed in *Sex and the City*. You were Carrie and I was some girl at a party and I was like, *I'm you, or, I will be when I turn thirty.*"

"Do you think it came true?" Jamie-as-Sarah-Michelle asked.

"Maybe, but in a fucked-up way where no one's casting us," said Ry-as-SJP.

"Maybe it's just that I'm Buffy and you're Carrie forever, like, no one can get over that," suggested Jamie-as-Sarah-Michelle.

"I wish we could be Buffy and Carrie forever."

"We could have a spin-off show."

"Middle-aged Buffy Summers and Carrie Bradshaw have retired to Los Angeles where they fight demons in Manolo Blahniks," said Ry-as-SJP.

"Carrie's perpetual inability to help but wonder could be really useful in solving demonic crime," Jamie-as-Sarah-Michelle said.

"Or we could share a house and let our blond grow out and start making matzo ball soup, just become Carrie and Buffy as full-on Jewish matriarchs."

"It will be good for the kids to be raised by Buffy and Carrie, I think," said Jamie.

"Will it?" Ry asked. "I mean, part of me worries Carrie just perpetuates a fantasy that you can be a navel-gazey writer and still end up with a closet full of thousand-dollar shoes."

"But she's getting the rich boyfriends to pay for them, right?" said Jamie.

"No," Ry said. "It's credit card debt. Carrie's, like, a true romantic with no head for finances."

"Buffy has a shrewder head on her shoulders, I think," Jamie said. "She's willing to take a service-industry job when she needs one. Her fashion's a little basic, but at least she lives within her means. The kids will be okay."

Jamie and Ry felt giddy as they picked shoes and then pleather halters for Jamie-as-Sarah-Michelle-Gellar, as they chose leggings, tulle, scarves, headpieces, stick-on flowers, bra tops, and sequin jumpsuits for Ry-as-Sarah-Jessica.

"They're gonna have a really fabulous life as platonic co-parents," Ry said.

"Sarah Jessica, with your eyes and that bedazzled bustier,

is gonna turn every head in the Whole Foods snack aisle," said Jamie.

"Should we just keep calling each other Sarah?" Jamie asked on the train home.

"Sure, Sarah," Ry said.

"I feel like this is how I want to make art forever," Jamie said. "Art with no product. I mean, I guess we have these photos but that's not the whole thing."

"I like that," said Ry. "Art with no audience. Pretending we're in a play."

At the house, Manny was ready to go to dinner, shirt tucked and hair salt-sprayed up.

"Wanna see our pictures?" Jamie asked and immediately started fanning them out, telling Manny about the hotness of being Sarah Schulman, and the Buffy/Carrie spin-off where blond Jewish women raise kids and fight demon crime.

Ry laughed hysterically the whole time. Manny looked confused.

"There was a machine in the back of the mall," Ry explained, "and it turned us into Sarahs." Ry kept laughing.

"Why are you talking like that?" Manny asked. "Are you still Sarahs?"

Ry realized their voice was high and nasally, a combination of SJP and Sarah Silverman. They were still Sarahs. And Manny was still Manny. Ry fell silent.

"So where do you want to go to dinner?" Jamie asked. "Ry and I were thinking maybe noodles?"

"Maybe noodles," repeated Manny. "You gonna change?" she asked Ry.

Manny followed Ry down the hall into the bedroom and shut the door.

"Were you going to ask whether Jamie could come to dinner?" Manny asked.

"They're our guest," Ry said.

"They're not our guest," said Manny. "They're some poet who needed a place to crash and now you've decided to be their BFF."

"Okay, what do you suggest happens next?" Ry asked.

"Tell Jamie the truth," Manny said. "We had plans."

"I can't," said Ry.

Manny stared at Ry, holding their ground.

"It's Jamie's last night!" Ry had emergency feelings.

Ry began to cry. Why was Ry such a baby?

"Jesus, Ry," Manny said.

Ry went into the bathroom and shut the door.

Manny, she thought, was putting her in an impossible position. Sometimes, Ry thought, you had to make decisions based on the allegiances of your heart in the moment, and if those were going to disrupt your home, well, you'd just have to make a new home. Ry would go to dinner with Jamie! They would get giant bowls of noodles and make bad theater and imagine worlds outside of capitalism and gentrification! They would go to Utah where Jamie lived and climb rocky spires into the sky and resist the pull of homonormativity forever! Then sickness overcame Ry. Ugh, Ry thought, the fear of losing home was so primal.

Ry looked into the mirror, put their shoulders back and

relaxed their hips. They met their own gaze. They put some gel in their hair and made it stand a little taller in the front.

Ry could see that in the *Girls Just Want to Have Fun* exchange, they were the girl with the true secret passion, expressed through poems, which made Jamie the cool, adventurous girl who could see Ry's amazingness, who would whisk Ry out from under Daddy's thumb.

And that meant Manny had to be Daddy.

But Manny wasn't Daddy.

Ry could see it now, they kept casting Manny as Daddy so they'd have something easy to rebel against, when it was *the gentrified city* who was Daddy.

A new inner voice popped into Ry's head: *bullies often conceptualize themselves as under attack when they are the ones originating the pain.* It was Sarah Schulman's voice, somehow just in there now. *Ugh*, Ry didn't want to be a bully.

Ry's problem, Ry thought, is they kept forgetting which movie they were in.

Ry penciled in their brows decisively and met their newly less-penetrable gaze.

Ry came out of the bathroom and into the bedroom.

Manny was sitting on the bed. Ry pushed down Manny's shoulders and jutted a knee between Manny's thighs and kissed Manny's mouth. Manny smiled shyly, tentatively, like they wanted to make sure they could trust something good was happening. Ry wedged their hand past Manny's belt and into Manny's boxer briefs, putting just a little pressure where pressure mattered, kissed Manny again, hard. Still lying on their back, Manny reached for Ry with both arms. Ry lifted their head just an inch and said, "Come on, boo boo, let's go get pizza."

Manny smiled. They loved pizza. "And Jamie?"

"Jamie will be fine," said Ry. "I'll just say I forgot we had a thing we had to go to."

Manny squeezed Ry's hand and smiled. They looked like a teenage dancer nerd about to sneak out the window with their boyfriend, like a tiny blue Pegasus with orange bangs, like a big-eyed chubby pastel hamster, like something, Ry thought, very cute.

GOSSIP

Since their names are Evan and Ada, let's get out of the way that they actually look Edenic. Evan has this unkempt-but-enlightened face, all ensconced in flowing waves (from above) and wiry curls (starting from the chin and jawline). He looks undernourished and glowing, the way a man would look if he were on the kind of pre-fire raw vegan diet we think we all imagine they had in the Garden of Eden. And Ada, her body's all big, smooth curves. Ada has that barefoot-and-pregnant look, even with red lipstick on, and her hair of course is long curls.

But the reversal of their names makes sense, too, Adam-and-Eve-wise, Cass says: "Evan's the curious one, listening to snakes and putting things in his mouth while Ada wants to name all the animals, to claim everything as hers."

What happened is they were friends, kind of, then they dated for a few weeks, starting on Christmas Day, and then they broke up.

*   *   *

When they met, in June of that year, they had this instant physical thing. Evan and Ada both felt an intense pull, and, even though they weren't each other's type, both of them were the kind of people to think this meant something. Ada believed in reincarnation, which made her trust that a pull meant unfinished business, something important to learn or explore. Evan believed, simply, in listening to what the body says it wants.

Evan was a masseur. The first time they met, Minhee says, Evan massaged Ada's head at a party and it made her wish her head were detachable and could live with Evan's hand forever. After that when they ran into each other, they'd cuddle, ostentatiously and disgustingly, without talking much or thinking about sex. They had friends in common, so they'd run into each other a lot. They cuddled at art shows, at movies, at diners. We all thought it was weird, and a little gross. But they were both unbalanced, Evan and Ada, and when they cuddled, Evan told Cori, they were filled with a neutral calm.

"Do you think that means you're in love with her?" Cori had asked.

Evan shook his head. "No, I mean, I like seeing her, but it's not like I want anything specific from her," he said.

Still, when Cori had a small gathering on Christmas, weeks later, she invited both Evan and Ada, curious to see what might happen. According to Cori, who likes math and weird facts, Christmas is the day people have the most sex because the annual onslaught of Christmas songs and movies makes people desperate for love. If things were going to go further between Evan and Ada, Cori thought, Christmas was the time.

At the party, everyone played Taboo and Scattergories, drank champagne cocktails and ate frosted cookies Cori had made, and then at some point, Ada sprawled herself across a loveseat in the corner of Cori's apartment, drunk and sleepy with smeared lipstick. Evan approached, asking if Ada felt okay. Ada nodded, but pressed her head against Evan's thigh like a cat, and Evan started massaging her head instinctually. During the head massage, Ada tilted her head back and gazed at Evan, and something happened inside of this gaze. It was like the gaze created a little glowy bubble around them and they wanted the bubble to grow bigger, brighter, totally encompassing. Or like the gaze allowed them inside each other, a little, and this made them want to be inside each other completely. Ada flung her head and shoulders farther over the back of the couch and then reached her hand behind her, wrapping it around the back of Evan's neck. Those of us who watched felt Ada was like quicksand, like a fairy-tale tree with suddenly active limbs, like something that looked inert but was frighteningly active. Sarah rolled her eyes at these descriptions, though: "Most people just aren't very sexy," Sarah said. "Ada is, and it apparently makes people so jealous they need to compare her to landscapes."

But so, Evan was easily seduced by Ada's gaze, by her unfurling, languorous movements, by her coffin-shaped nails digging just a little into Evan's scalp as she kissed his mouth. Evan came home with Ada then, and more or less stayed there for a month, until Evan felt a little too tightly wrapped in Ada's too-active limbs, and wrested free.

Still, stuff happened between the initial seduction and Evan's bolting. Here's a recap of the stuff we know: they went to Ada's after Cori's Christmas party and had sex. Starting the day after the sex, Evan began to call after work to ask if Ada wanted to get dinner. She usually did. We all saw them together, eating huge bowls of vermicelli noodles or feeding each other diner pie. They started turning up at shows together, where Ada would stand silent and lipsticked at Evan's side, looking just past us like she was only half there, in a world with only her brain and the music, but when she talked to Evan, we could see her tune in to the world he occupied.

Once, they were at a daytime performance and some of us invited them to drinks after. Ada and Evan agreed they were tired, and drove to Ada's. At Ada's, they stripped down and had sex and then Evan took kale and garlic and frozen tilapia from Ada's fridge and made dinner. Ada opened cheap red wine and poured some.

"I'm glad we didn't go out for drinks," Evan said. "I'm glad we came home."

The night they broke up, Evan brought Ada to Oscar's goth-themed party. Everyone was there with powdered faces and black gauze veils. Ada wore a corset and a tutu and black glitter nail polish and lots of turquoise eye shadow. Evan wore black eyeliner and a black T-shirt, but this was transformative. We're sure you can imagine—starved enlightened hippie dude to gaunt goth prince. When Evan came to pick Ada up, she was already ready and he said, "You look amazing." Then he said, "It makes me nervous how much time you spend trying to please me." This part of the story irritates Minhee, who says Ada's idea of an entire fun Saturday night is staying in and listening to music, doing her makeup, dressing up, and taking selfies. "Like, appreciate that about Ada, or don't," Minhee says, "but don't think she's doing it for you, dude." The night of the goth party, Ada had pre-sharpened her pencils, psyched to line Evan's eyes on the couch before they left, but he'd brought his own eyeliner, still in its packaging, and insisted on applying it himself.

Then Evan ignored Ada at the party. Ada looked over and Evan didn't look back, as though he'd forgotten he'd brought her there. Ada got drunk off dark and stormys while she talked to other people they both knew, looking over at Evan, who never turned his eyes to make contact.

Ada went out for a cigarette with Sol who said, "Evan can be a space cadet. Don't bring it up. Bringing stuff up too soon always fucks everything."

So when they got home to Ada's, Ada didn't bring it up. Instead of bringing it up, she asked Evan to tighten her corset. "Tighter," she kept demanding, until her body was making little gasps. Evan kept asking was she okay. Ada was okay. She said so. She put her knees on the couch, and her wrists. Her ass was really close to Evan's face, which was leaning over to see the laces as he pulled. "Fuck me, please," Ada gasped, when the corset was sufficiently tight, when she could barely inhale. "With your hand." So Evan did, using the hand that was not pulling the corset's laces. Ada screamed a lot. Her screams were guttural. Then she stopped screaming, because it felt like the hand that was fucking her was not connected to a body. Like she was being fucked by a disembodied hand. She turned her face. Evan's eyes were blank and bored and dead. "Are you okay?" Ada asked. It was weird, for a person with her ass in the air to ask this, but also appropriate. It's appropriate to ask a dead-eyed lover if they're okay.

"I don't think I'm as into this as you are," Evan said.

"Oh," Ada said.

"We can stop," Ada said.

"Okay. Let's stop," said Evan.

So they stopped. They were sitting next to each other on the couch. Ada's tights were still pulled down and her tutu angled ridiculously up, so it was just her bare ass on the fuzzy cushion of the flowered Goodwill couch. Her corset loosened with no hand holding it. She tried to caress Evan's shoulder. Evan didn't feel dead, but he felt absent, like he was trying to will his own absence from his body. To give his body generously to Ada, but to disappear from it himself.

"I just," Evan said. "The look in your eyes just now was really intense. Like, really emotional."

"Oh," Ada said. She said it in a wounded way. She took her hand off Evan's shoulder.

Evan said, "Like, until now, I thought we were experiencing things at the same emotional level. But now it's clear that you are experiencing more emotions than me."

Right then, Ada was experiencing a lot of emotions.

"This is from a look on my face?"

"Yeah. Your face had, like, the most emotional look on anyone's face I've ever seen." Evan tried to describe the face in his head. Ada's eyes were normally amber and blue but the blue and amber in Ada's eyes had mixed into pure, even green and this appeared to be a result of a desire so strong it made everything in Ada distill and open. She looked aching and hungry and so vulnerable it disgusted him. Basically, Sol pointed out, Ada had become the Eve. "That's the whole point of that story: guys only like you if you hide your hunger. Like, guys just mostly aren't that hungry—that's why they need Burger King commercials to tell them they're only a real man if they muster hunger." Sol took a long sip of her tequila soda. "You ever notice that shit? How every food commercial geared toward men has to *convince* them they're starving, and every food commercial for women is trying to assure them that a hundred calorie cup of Yoplait is actually the same fucking thing as banana cream pie?"

But so, back to Ada and Evan on the couch: "The most emotional look on anyone's face?" Ada shrieked. She was sounding really emotional now, we're sure, her voice high-pitched and about to break. Black and turquoise tears rolled down Ada's cheeks.

Evan was retreating more and more. To Ada, his face looked pitying and repulsed.

Ada tugged at her tights like a three-year-old who doesn't know how to pull up her own tights and stayed bare-assed.

"I have to go," Evan said.

"You have to go?" Ada screamed. "I am the one with a bare ass here, the one who was getting fucked here! Fuck you, Evan."

"It's just, I feel repelled."

"You feel repulsed?"

"Repelled."

"What the fuck." Ada had sob-voice now, which only repulsed Evan further. "Evan!"

But Evan was already gone. She could see it. She rubbed her face into the flowered couch cushion smearing black and turquoise makeup all over her face and it.

While she was still facedown and snotting and rubbing, he said they'd talk soon and walked toward and out the door.

*   *   *

But this is not the whole story. It's not that Evan left just because of a look in Ada's eyes. Something else had to be going on. Lissa, who hooked up with Evan for a while, says it might make more sense if you know that Evan is a hippie, when it comes down to it, and Ada is not. Lissa says that for Evan, sex is about the essential masculine and the essential feminine yin-yanging together. About whole-making. About putting the little yang dot in the yin and the yin dot in the yang—about exchange. Evan liked the idea of swapping parts, of letting parts mingle, meld together, slowly. The sex Evan liked was gentle missionary.

"That's so disgusting," Minhee says, swirling her vodka and lavender cocktail. "Hippies are gross, they're like the straightest of all straight people. They have to bring the fantasy of yin-yang sex, of magical baby-making into every fucking interaction." Minhee says Ada thinks you get to decide who brainwashes you and she's chosen the queer theorists, because who wants to think of herself as yin? According to Minhee, Ada thinks everyone who wants to should get to do the fucking. She thinks everyone who wants to should get to be a beautiful object.

Sarah says that, when she was Ada's lover, there was a lot of thigh-riding and nipple-grinding, there was strap-on exchange and hitting. Sarah says sex for Ada is a place for the couple, or group, whatever, to express their individualities, to communicate stuff where language would fail, to each other and themselves. Ada told some of us, though, that she enjoyed Evan's gentle missionary sex and sweet licking foreplay. It felt like a way of knowing Evan, of experiencing his desires, and she liked Evan.

But, Minhee points out, when Ada showed Evan her double-sided cock, he seemed interested, and she was relieved. "I never really trusted it, though," says Minhee, drawing on a smoke. "Evan was just into the idea of something experimental, fun, quote-unquote gender-bending and, like, transgressive."

But, we think, with this corset-tightening, with this ass-in-the-air humiliation, Ada was showing Evan something about her. It was Ada's Desires Time. Evan could see that Ada's desires were not just about transgressive fun, that somehow this breath-restriction, this humiliation, had lubed up Ada's connective potential, cleared something out of the way and now Ada was asking Evan, with those pulsing all-green eyes, to connect with her dark parts. It was too much.

"Bitches can't be hungry," Sol reiterates.

Jaden says, though, that Sol's wrong about male hunger. "Testosterone makes guys super hungry, actually. It's that they're mostly not curious," Jaden says. "They'll eat, just, whatever. Ada, like Eve, wants to find strange fruit and put it in her mouth. Cis guys always think they want girls like that, but ultimately they do not."

But Lissa insists that Evan is just someone who values independence. Evan had thought Ada valued independence, too, Lissa says, because early in their courtship, they went to the mountains to hike to a waterfall and Ada had insisted on hiking to the waterfall from boulder to boulder in the creek, rather than on the path alongside it, even though Evan was on the path. She then lay topless on a smooth rock emerging from the river, and watched the water, barely looking at Evan, but seeming totally content. "It seems kind of painful, if you ask me," Lissa says, holding her white wine like she was making a toast, "to be ditched by your date for a river. But Evan chose to see Ada as independent, as someone romantic and free who loved whimsically and then wanted to frolic alone in the trees."

Minhee laughs. "I remember hearing about that day. Ada was having a hard time because she was thinking a lot about her ex," Minhee says. Sarah perks up and Minhee says, "Sorry, honey, not you." Minhee says Ada had woken up concerned about how long she could stay in this gentle missionary sex routine. "You know Ada's not running through the river ignoring you because everything's going great, boy," says Minhee. "God, guys are such idiots."

The goth party was the first time Evan could sense Ada's anxiety, Ada's desire to be pet and entertained. He saw her across the room, a corseted and excessively—suddenly grotesquely—made-up sea creature locating him with her eyes, reaching with her sticky glittered tentacles, wanting to ensnare. Evan didn't want to be ensnared. He wanted to be two free and separate creatures who met occasionally to refuel, to cuddle at a party, to frolic in the woods, to fuck gently in missionary position.

But okay, let's go back to the look in Ada's eyes, because the heat, the intensity, mattered. At least according to Christopher, who's sort of a crazy cat man, but whose perspective we won't totally discount. When cats go into heat, Christopher says, they claw into the carpet and crawl, rear hoisted and yowling. They'll do this for days despite sleepiness and hunger and absence of any suitable partner. "We've developed culture," Christopher says, "a whole system of traffic lights and schools and poetry and etiquette manuals, so that we're not all bloody from scraping our chests along sidewalks or rubbing our bottom fluids on each other's legs." So heat comes out weirdly, says Christopher, often as teary breakdowns or sheer misplaced rage.

Sarah though, says that while some heat might manifest as rage or tears, sure, Ada's heat mainly manifests as heat. "It's super hot," Sarah says, smirking and draining her IPA.

"Well, whatever," says Christopher, setting down his bitters and soda. "Culture hasn't made room for heat, however it comes out, and so people find it scary. I mean, it's like all the girl-feelings the whole of culture has tried to repress, rearing its head from the darkest under-the-bed place. I mean, I personally find my cat's heat scary, too, but I just stick a Q-Tip in there and we're done."

Jaden says Ada had cried over her former lover for 238 days. ("Not you, honey," Minhee says again to perked-up Sarah.) Ada's body was demanding *Evan Evan Evan* but her heart was asking for a latex sheath, steel armor. Ada's heart could see that Evan's heart was a changeling. Ada's heart could see this in Evan's irritability, in his occasional extreme torpor. "But Ada's a cerebral person," Jaden says. "She's not always willing to acknowledge what her heart can see."

Sarah has additional info to contribute, which is that Ada has a problem where, when she gets drunk and has sex, she slips in time. It's the combination of drinking and the arousal-to-orgasm cycle that renders clocks impotent, makes Ada get unstuck. Like, one time, shit-faced on vodka, Ada started screaming at Sarah and bawling because, while Sarah was fucking Ada in the present time, Ada was being fucked by a manipulative dude punk bassist ten years prior. This was literally true, Sarah insisted, and not some metaphor. "If it were me," Sarah says, "I just wouldn't have drunk sex, but Ada's not great at making rules for herself."

And what didn't help Ada stay fixed in time, Jaden pointed out, was that she was wearing the corset she bought during her relationship with her former lover ("Not you, Sarah, *god,*" says Minhee), the corset she wore for their fancy nights out to Rasputina concerts and experimental circuses. The lover had pulled Ada's laces tighter and tighter, watched breathing become a challenge with each small tug, kissed Ada's face or fingered her collarbone at each widening of Ada's eyes. Ada had put eyeliner on the former lover, and this lover, too, for their nights out, had become a gaunt, goth prince. "I can totally see how the corset, plus the breath-restriction play, would ease Ada's slippage in time," Jaden says.

And so, if what Sarah says is true, then the look Ada gave Evan in that moment contained three years' worth of complicated emotions; it was a look of deep love and mourning not meant for him at all.

Unconsciously, Evan knew the look wasn't even meant for him, and this hurt.

But so, here is what really happened, probably, if you believe that rule that the simplest explanation is usually the right one. At the goth party, one of the people Evan was talking to was Marion. Marion was this really young, just-out-of-college person with an easy, neutral face, a bouncy ponytail, and hairy legs. Marion was likable and not unbalanced. She was wearing a simple black dress and black lipstick and looked like a convincing goth but also like a nice girl with costumey lip-stick. Marion and Evan talked about politics and Evan started thinking how not unbalanced Marion was. He looked in her eyes and they didn't spark and they weren't hungry. They were present and attentive and clear. Evan looked over at Ada and she looked so crazy. She looked like the first woman who ever slipped in time just after eating the forbidden fruit and arriving frazzled and guilty in the twenty-first century where she promptly styled herself like a Fraggle. He looked back at Marion. Marion looked sweet and normal and like someone who would have a job that helped people and who your mom would like.

Later, when Ada was bent over the couch with her ass in the air, what Evan thought was that Marion wouldn't want to have weird degrading sex like this. All that happened was Evan started to have a crush on someone else.

Still, we don't know for sure about any of this. We think it's all true, or maybe none of it. There are other theories, too, of course—Cass thinks Scorpio and Sag are simply incompatible, and Vic just shrugs and says Ada's crazy. You should just ask Ada—she's such an oversharer, she'll probably tell you every-thing. Or ask Evan—you might be able to figure something out by the way his hands move when he tells you his curt version, by the moment in your inquiry when his eyes can't make contact.

Or, you know, invent something that makes more sense than what's here—you know Evan and Ada, too, or at least you know people who are enough like them that your story might work, that it might, even, be the most correct.

BECOMING TREES

It began in the season when everyone was changing: Tam was straight now with a kid and Mo was a sudden leather daddy and Oscar had new pecs and facial hair. Even our one gay friend, Luca, seemed to have become a permanent resident of a phone-based app which allowed him to live as a thirty-years-younger wide-eyed cartoon dog. It seemed like everyone was wrapping themselves in chrysali and having late-in-life emergences as different kinds of creatures, and what this made clear was that we weren't becoming anything. We felt like caterpillars who didn't know that being a caterpillar wasn't the endgame. We felt like foamy pond water.

We whispered about it in our houses at night. We had made peace with childlessness during the previous decade—we'd felt ready to wrinkle and sag, to day drink and cackle, to become wry hags at the time before the end of the world. But one day Oscar said he didn't want to have "old dyke face" and the phrase infected us. We looked in the mirror and whereas we'd previously thought phrases like "silver fox" and "weathered femme" and "daddy" we now thought "old dyke face."

Oscar came over with a suitcase of button-ups he'd grown out of. "My lesbian shirts," he said. It was a good collection. We oohed over Oxford collars and checked ourselves out in American Apparel pink. We hadn't worn pink since childhood. "You guys look good," Oscar said, but his biceps—so taut and shiny!—pushed at the seams of his T-shirt and we knew he was just being nice.

Later that night, we were eating veggie burgers and drinking beer we'd bottled ourselves, using a microbrew set Jan got as a birthday gift. Our cat, Judy, was chasing a lizard, pouncing on it and setting it free over and over again. We let her have this little connection to wildness, even though it was gross to clean up later. Jan announced that she was concerned about gender. "I mean, there are only two options," she said. "I'm not thrilled with either of them, but that's what we've got." Before Jan was a tree, people paid her to remodel things. She'd knock out one ceiling and replace it with a whole other ceiling; she'd transform hideous drywall into exposed wood beams. She made beautiful dressers out of planks. What Jan did seemed like magic. She hadn't taken a bunch of humanities classes or anything, and I found this hot, Jan's irritation with abstraction, her impatience with anything that wasn't immediately applicable, her ability to reshape without reading a bunch of books first. But sometimes I'd end up butchsplaining to her, I knew, and that night, what I butchsplained were binaries. I used an analogy, the way I did when I was a teacher. "Black and white is an example of a false binary," I said, "because there's gray."

"Gray is still just black and white, Sarah," said Jan. "But you can add some purple to gray. Color is much more dynamic."

I had nothing to say to that.

"You sound like my dad," I said, and went to brush my teeth.

Jan yelled after me, "I'm concerned about the future!"

I knew what she meant. We were the sort of dykes who had believed in The Future Is Female. We believed in a future in which women used soft power to stop men from using their phallic drills to siphon the earth's blood, to plumb nonconsensually into it and steal its powerful black energy-juice in order to make their penisy Lamborghinis go faster. We dreamed about offices of women employing men and paying them good wages to make the things we wanted them to make—windmills and an electric light-rail to replace the highway system and high-quality mattresses in three varieties of firmness that our female-run government would supply to every citizen. "Maybe in the future," I said, climbing into bed, "everyone will have severe bowl cuts and strap their feet with pleather into big wooden blocks."

"People are already doing that," Jan said. "Maybe they'll stand on giant sponges."

"Then they'll soak everything up."

"I think that would be nice," Jan said. "If people soaked more things up."

This is how we talked, when we were people still, when we lay together under down comforters and laundered sheets that smelled like organic lavender-scented detergent. I can see the washing machine now, from the place where I'm becoming a tree. It's still there, covered in a layer of dust so thick that the dust looks like a soft mat where creatures from the insect kingdom lie down for naps. Do I miss laundered sheets? Yes, I miss them. But that night:

"I don't want to become a man or a woman," Jan whispered in her sleep voice. Sometimes when Jan was mostly asleep was when she said the things that were very important and so I had to be careful to ask questions gently.

"What do you want to become?" I asked, rubbing her back with light pressure.

"A tree," Jan whispered, grinning. She started laughing then, big weird ha ha ha laughter, and then snoring. I required an ever-changing combination of eye pillows and creams, melatonin supplements and scalding baths, but Jan was always able to snore out of nowhere, to slip easily into a world I was terrified, for no reason, to enter.

When Jan said that, though, I realized my heart had been scrunched up tight in my chest, because right then it expanded. It made me think of those plastic capsules, the ones you'd put into water and they'd turn into dinosaur sponges. So that was how it started. My heart turned into a dinosaur sponge.

The next morning, when I went out to water the plants, I looked at them differently. All their little leaves bounced. I watched as Judy sidled the perimeter of a patch of mint. I watered tomatoes, peonies, oregano, basil, summer squash. The plants seemed full of conflicting desires. They wanted to burrow into the cool black loam and also to reach into the sun. They wanted to keep their process secret in a tight little bud and then unfurl all at once, pink and glorious. I'd always felt pressured to identify as an introvert or an extrovert. As butch or femme. I never got over wanting to have my cake and eat it, too. No one told the plants they had to be one thing or another. I slipped off my sandals and stood barefoot in the garden. I imagined the soles of my feet growing little hairs, then tentacles that reached down and multiplied outward. Suddenly, I had never wanted anything so much.

"Why do you want to become a tree?" I asked Jan later that night, in bed.

"I don't know," Jan said. "There just aren't as many options for how to be human as people think."

"I want to be one, too," I said.

"You do?" Jan said.

"Yes," I said, pulling her head onto my chest.

"But you want to be everything," she sighed.

We watched YouTube videos of people who had successfully become trees. There were so many factors that needed to be considered: diversity of microbes in the soil, successful chloroplast growth and functioning, readiness to give up identity. Identity, the videos said, had previously been the key to our sense of well-being—whether our individuality was being recognized and affirmed. Being a tree, affirmation would feel different. Love would feel different. We would be happiest if our soil was full of microbes chatting. We would be happiest if the soil was rich enough to contain a complex fungal network that would allow us to sort of blur into it and talk to or just sort of be each other.

We learned, in a video with computerized diagrams, that human chloroplast growth was modeled after sea slugs, who learned to live off sunlight like plants by stealing chloroplasts from the algae around them. Even as a human, I always felt confused by diagrams, but it seemed that the sea slugs ate the algae and found some way to incorporate the algae's chloroplasts into their own bodies, becoming part plant.

We watched a time-lapse video of a planted woman becoming a tree, her green human skin growing a shell of fibers and then smooth bark, her torso and legs growing solid and cylindrical, her long black hair becoming waved then papery then leaves. She looked peaceful throughout the process, and then she looked like a tree, like any other tree.

We ordered a kit.

In bed, I asked Jan if she knew the myth of Daphne and Apollo.

"I don't know any myths, Bear," said Jan.

"Can I tell you?" I asked, a little worried about butchsplaining again.

"Yeah," said Jan, flopping her head into my armpit. "But rub my head, too."

"Okay," I said. Judy was curled up against my other side, and so I petted Judy with one hand and Jan with the other. "So, Apollo, who's the god of wisdom, makes fun of Cupid's arrow-shooting skills. In response, Cupid gets really mad and shoots Apollo."

"Mmm," said Jan.

"Janny, don't fall asleep. Listen. So Apollo's been shot by Cupid's arrow and so he's just gonna fall hardcore in love with the first girl he sees, and that girl happens to be this river nymph Daphne."

"Why's it always gotta be a girl?" Jan asked, already with sleep voice.

"So Apollo's chasing Daphne through the forest. She's running and running and crying because she wants to die a virgin."

"She's a dyke?" said Jan, interested now.

"Probably," I said. "And so Daphne's like screaming and begging for help from the river god and finally when Apollo's just about to be able to tackle her, the river god turns Daphne into a tree."

"Can't rape a tree," Jan said and immediately started snoring.

I pulled her hair a little. "Janny!" I said.

"Ow, I'm awake," said Jan. "I heard you. It's a fucked-up story. Two dudes fighting over their shooting skills aka cock size and this poor river bitch Daphne just happens to be there."

"I know," I said. "It's like everything."

We planted an extensive vegetable garden to nourish us during the time before we would develop chloroplasts, and to nourish the soil. This was strongly recommended in the reading materials that came with our kits. If we ate from our dirt, we'd thrive better once we lived there. We ordered seeds from a queer anarchist seed collective and planted sunflowers, kale, rainbow chard, beets, corn, lima beans. After depositing the last of the seeds in the dirt, I approached the trees slowly and whispered, "I'm going to be one of you soon." I put my ear against the bark of a kumquat tree to see if it had anything to say to me, but it did not. I picked a kumquat and ate it whole, but it didn't have anything to say either. We waited as the seeds we buried developed their desires and plans. We waited as they grew parts that pushed through the dirt toward the sun and breathed in carbon dioxide and made fruit and all that.

While our garden took root, we went to a silent meditation retreat, to practice not speaking. The first couple of days, it was hard not to talk. When a stupid thought popped into one of our minds, like, *Did we remind our cat-sitter that Judy won't eat unless there is food in the very center of the bowl, that you have to shake her dry food around?*, it was very difficult not to ask each other for reassurance, and when a deep feeling popped into one of our minds, like, *My mother didn't mean to be a smothering and needy monster, she was just really damaged by the patriarchy*, it was very difficult not to tell the other person, but on day six, it was magically easy. Worlds can be made in six days, I realized, and then slipped easily back into meditation, not feeling the need to tell Jan.

When I looked at Jan, though, I began to feel we were somehow both seeing each other more clearly and becoming greater mysteries to one another, that we were somehow both more multiply connected and more autonomous. We glanced at each other and wandered simultaneously outside. In front of a yawning elm we stopped, faced the sun, and felt our bodies arc toward it like bows. It wasn't freedom we felt. We felt almost puppeted from our chests but it felt so good, to be pulled.

We'd become other kinds of things—so quickly, we marveled, on the car ride home—things who felt a little tapped into the way tongueless creatures understood things.

On the way home, we stopped to see the sequoias. The sequoias always made me feel emotional, the size of them and their age. They were three thousand years old and some of them showed the history of their trauma, hollowed out centers and thick black scars. I threw myself against a sequoia trunk. Its top layer of bark was thick and furred, yielding a little to my chest.

At home, we tossed a tinfoil ball around for Judy, ordered a pizza, opened some saisons that had been waiting in the fridge, and discussed the house. Our city was in a housing crisis and we could not ethically let ours stand empty. Besides, it would be good to have someone living in the house in case anything went horribly wrong and we needed to be dug up and hospitalized or in case our sprinkler system broke and we needed to be watered.

We remembered Oscar was looking for a new place.

We texted. We were, more and more, becoming a "we," a unit that took actions without conferring first, instead knowing things at the same time.

After a long conversation over home-brewed stouts, it was decided: Oscar would move in and live rent-free, be our caretaker in exchange. If anything happened upon which we needed to be moved, replanted, healed, or tended to, he could use our 401Ks. If nothing happened and he was old, he could use our 401Ks, too.

"God, now I need to have a kid," Oscar said. "To be your tree parent after I'm gone."

"Don't," I said. "Your kid is just going to starve or burn to death in the apocalypse."

"Plus you're too old," Jan said. "Maybe Tam's kid."

"Yeah, maybe Lavender," Oscar agreed. "He's very caring and tender already."

Jan and I looked at each other and, via our meditation-retreat-established silent communication, expressed the weight of realizing we might live for a very very long time.

"If we're still here by then," I said, "we'll probably be pretty self-sufficient."

"True," Oscar said. "But y'all still need a midwife." He sipped his stout. "I'm totally your man."

We ate our crops. We discovered that eating raw corn is pleasurable, that it creates huge amounts of corn-foam in your mouth, which builds like starchy shampoo. We planted lemon balm and sage, just to smell them as we changed. We drank chlorophyll-infused water from our local health food store. We bought chlorophyll from Amazon and mixed it into everything, smoothies in the morning and pesto at night.

As the video predicted, we started worrying about our identities.

"I feel like I'm a pansy at heart," I said. "And maybe I never got to fully express that, the way the kids are doing now. Like, I felt like I had to be femme, and then I felt like I wanted to be butch, but maybe I should be wearing, like, pastel lipstick and a single earring?"

"That would look cute on you," said Jan. "Do you want to go to the mall?"

So we went to the mall and I settled on a matte teal lipstick, applied by a wonderful boy with orange eye shadow and a smear of gold glitter on one cheek, who I loved immediately.

For my earring, I chose a silver triangle dangling at the end of a long chain.

"I love this look on you," Jan said back at home. "Pansy Bear."

But then I got sad. "I want to live life like this now," I said.

"This isn't a life," Jan said. "It's a lipstick."

But after Jan went to bed that night, I snuck into the bathroom and reapplied my lipstick, put on my earring, and admired my fresh barber cut. I felt tough and soft in a whole new way.

We built a tall fence behind the house so that the neighbors would be protected from the knowledge that we were out back becoming trees. Jan built a separate walkway so that our visitors wouldn't bother Oscar. We emailed our friends and our families. *We are becoming trees,* we said. *Feel free to visit us by entering the side gate and walking down the path into our newly gated backyard. Please do not disrupt the tenants.* We added this last because we did not want Oscar having to manage the feelings of our angry sisters and weeping mothers. If he wanted to go outside and show and tell us, that could be his choice.

Our mothers did weep and said we had a death wish and our sisters did yell and call us selfish. *How were we going to be strong role models to our little nieces if we were covered in bark,* one shouted. *Weren't we aware of all the fighting that'd been done so women might have a voice and now we were going to give up our mouths,* shouted another. *Like Hello Kitty,* yelled a third.

"They weren't that happy when we were using our mouths," said Jan.

It was so true. We'd heard about our selfishness and death wishes and overall idiocy from our families, but we were a little surprised when our friends also felt betrayed. We got it, though, too. Everyone was sober and morphing and our house had become a safe space for dykes who wanted to have drinks and talk shit. We were taking that away.

The morning after we sent the email, our friend Elana appeared at our door. Jan was at work, so it was just me, but Elana was mostly my friend anyhow. "You guys really don't need to do this," she said. It was the same thing I remembered her saying to Oscar. That was a thing about Elana, she wasn't very inquisitive. She thought she knew all the ways peoples' parental relationships and socioeconomic backgrounds and feelings mixed with their current situation in order to make them do exactly the thing they were doing now. Another thing about Elana though, was she always showed up. I'd seen a meme posted recently, probably by someone's mother, that said the only people you should befriend are the ones whose eyes light up when you talk about your dreams. Something like that. I'd enjoyed that meme, but also I thought it was good to keep people like Elana around, too, people who wanted you to stay just as you were, people who accepted your annoying tics and shortcomings. Plus it's hard when becoming the next version of yourself means leaving behind the ways and rituals of the people you've been growing with. I could understand that.

"I know I don't need to do this," I told Elana. "I just don't feel like I have anything else I want to do as a human," I said. "And, like, look I'm sick of the cancerous human spread." It wasn't exactly true but with people like Elana you had to sound surer than you were or they'd see your little gaps of uncertainty and jam their claws in there and twist your brain in the direction they wanted it to be thinking.

"Oh my god, is this a suicide?" Elana asked.

"No," I said. "I mean, I can't stop thinking about how underground is where actual real life is, I mean at least in the places where no one is sterilizing the soil for pesticide-free corn and doing that rapey fracking shit."

"Uch, *god*," Elana said. "You're going to be a *tree* and still you have to worry about white cis male violence."

I laughed. "You'll visit me?" I said.

"Uch, *yeah*," said Elana. "I mean, I get it. I'm sick of everything, too."

Somehow the phrase infected me. In bed that night, I asked Jan if she thought we were sick of everything and being Daphne-ish, just running away from the scary big bad world.

"I'm not scared of the world, Bear," said Jan. "I love the world." Jan smoothed my hair back and kept her hand on my forehead.

"Do you think we're making a mistake?"

"No," said Jan, "I want to do this *because* I love the world."

"And we're going to get to release oxygen into it and make energy from the sun and get intimate with it's little underground creatures." We'd been rehearsing this, and it was easy to grab back onto. "Okay," I said, "I just couldn't say all that to Elana."

"It's okay not to tell everybody everything, Bear," said Jan. She'd been saying that to me for years.

*　　*　　*

Jan and I pulled out the bed from the convertible couch and rewatched our favorite movies and ordered all the takeout we thought we'd miss. We read passages aloud from books we loved. We fed each other noodles and drank cans of sparkling water and felt Judy purring on our chests and waited, slowly greening.

One day, I woke up and Jan was much greener than she'd been. I removed the covers to observe her. Roots like tiny carrots protruded from the bottoms of her feet. She was so beautiful, I thought, human and green and rooting.

"Janny," I whispered, "you're almost ready."

"What about you?" she asked, her eyes still closed.

"Check me," I said.

"You're not green enough," said Jan. "You're sick-lez green. I'm pea-shoot green."

"Mm, pea shoots," I said.

We went to Chinatown to eat pea shoots for breakfast. In our city, people are creative and often appear in strange ways, like for art, and so it was okay that Jan had green skin and feet shaped like Japanese yams. I tried to get her to wear a witch hat to breakfast, but she pointed out that even if she had been dressed up as a witch earlier that morning, wouldn't she remove her hat before going to eat pea shoots? In the end, she wore a black denim jacket. We cuddled in a corner booth, two greenish dykes lifting chopsticks full of greasy leaves to each others' mouths.

"What if it's our last chance to eat noodles?" Jan asked. And so we ordered noodles, too, which arrived in a dry yellow nest, over which we poured a little gravy at a time in order to eat them part crispy, part soft, our favorite way.

We were full and tired and our plates were still heaping with food. Jan poked at my mouth with chopsticks full of pea shoots. "You need more chlorophyll," she insisted. And since I didn't know how much longer I'd be eating food like this, I opened my mouth for Jan's chopsticks again and again.

My nubby carrot roots grew. Bulbous and each with witch hairs, they made it difficult to walk. Jan was truly pea-colored now with roots long as wands.

Jan woke up increasingly more tired, and I helped her out into the sunshine, where she'd breathe deep and smile. Some of Jan's hair had turned into leaves and she'd sit there in the garden sometimes with her eyes closed and sometimes gazing at me. We were speaking less, though it was unclear whether we were losing our capacity for speech or just our desire to speak, and whether those things were even different after all.

Still, I worried: I didn't know how fast it would go from here. I texted Oscar and said I thought it was time for him to move in. He showed up that evening with a bag of clothes and stayed in our guest room.

We began sitting in the garden for most of the day. I sometimes foraged from the garden, shoving leaves into my mouth or sucking on a fallen kumquat, but Jan was making most of her own food, smiling spread-eagle in the dirt as her chloroplasts easily converted sun to sugar. When I stood in the dirt on my bulbed feet, I felt a feeling I'd never felt before, a cunty surge that went from my roots to the crown of my head and out like a beam.

* * *

169

Later, on our sofa bed I asked Jan, "Do you feel turned on, like, by the ground?"

"I don't know if that's the right word for it," Jan said. "But maybe literally turned on, like, activated."

"Maybe these are plant feelings," I said.

"They're plant feelings," echoed Jan. She started snoring. Judy purred.

One day, I woke up and it didn't feel like waking up. I felt different than an awake human. I felt, I guessed, like a tree. "Janny," I said. "Today is the day."

"Today is the day," Jan repeated. The repetition was like a spell, making it official.

When Oscar came into the living room, we told him, "Today is the day."

Our roots had grown too long and abundant to walk with. We no longer had anything that could properly be called "heels" or "balls of our feet." Oscar brought a wheelbarrow to the side of our sofa bed. We rolled into the barrow, one after the other and clutched each other, face-to-face and fetal. Oscar pushed us to the garden, deposited us onto our plot.

Out back in our new, gated area, Jan and I felt energized. We lay down and dug our fingers and then our palms into each other, our bodies writhing against the dirt. We pulled our hands out and plunged them, our five fingertips pressed together like little spades, into the soil, our slimy hands pushing into the hard clay earth and breaking it open. It was difficult to make the first crack into the clay, but as we drilled our fists down, the earth loosened. We let out little gasps of wonder and relief, and soon our arms were buried up past the elbows, and we moaned. We swirled our sticky hands around in bags of tree fertilizer, and pushed our fists into the earth again. I massaged the earth with one hand while pushing the other into Jan's body, and I could feel both the will and the surrender of each of the three of us, Jan, me, the earth. We were each pushing, each opening, taking more than we thought we could but relenting more, too. I felt Jan's wrist bone push into me just as the earth sucked my arm to the shoulder. Our legs were coated in slime and dirt, and Jan's legs were somehow buried to mid-calf. We kept writhing. It is so hard to plant anything.

But we pushed. We pummeled at the now receptive dirt, then wrapped our legs around one another and bore down. Our whole bodies were covered in mud and the sun beat hard. It was the best sex we'd had in years.

Underneath the soil, our roots are fusing. We're practicing passing chemicals back and forth, feelings and scents, and we can feel the neuralish root networks of the kumquat tree and the corn stalks creeping toward us and sniffing around in curiosity, and it's a friendly, benevolent feeling but mostly a feeling from a type of interaction that is unlike anything we would have felt as humans, an unnamable feeling that we are beginning to feel very interested in. Judy comes out and rubs against our legs, which are covered in stalky fibers, and purrs and it feels as though we purr back. When Oscar waters us we feel refreshed and suck up water through our feet-roots, but when it rains we feel amazing, like our bodies are becoming alive in places we didn't know about. The mushrooms around us are whispering and at first we can't hear them, but then we can and what we hear is that Mother Earth is dying, and that we are all working together to figure out how to revive her and I try to shout to Jan in the new way we're learning that we have to get out of here, that I need to go to the barber and put on my teal lipstick and tell everyone about the plan and Jan says Bear, baby, you don't have hair anymore, and they don't know how to listen yet anyway, and we can try to tell Oscar and Tam and Lavender, and baby just stay here, just stay here and do the work.

ALL THE TEENAGED SARAHS

THE ORDINARY WORLD

The ordinary world is a Midwest suburb built in the 1980s, made up of exactly three nearly identical architectural styles of houses.

Everyone has wall-to-wall beige carpet and teal throw pillows and a wall unit displaying blown-glass vases and miniature ladies with beanbag bodies and ceramic heads.

Sarah lives in the ordinary world.

Sarah rides her bike in the cul-de-sac. Sarah stands in the pantry and eats Cheez-Its straight from the box. Sarah reads very long series of books about girls who have more friends than she has.

The ordinary world is okay. It's whatever.

CALL TO ADVENTURE

On Sarah's twelfth birthday, she walks into her bedroom after school to find a towel covering a box-shaped object on her dresser, as though she's been gifted a sleeping bird. She knows this isn't actually the case, as her mother has expressed very clear disgust with animals who produce trays of poo, so under the towel is not a bird, but a small pink TV with a built-in VCR. Sarah would rather have a bird than a TV, but a TV is okay.

Sarah gets her tapes from downstairs and brings them upstairs to where the new TV is. She lays them out on the carpet and hovers her hand over the tapes like they are tarot cards, like she is Sarah in *The Craft*—Sarah feels basically and secretly interchangeable with all teenaged Sarahs—until her hand feels like it should grab one. It grabs. Without looking, Sarah flips up the little door of the VCR slot and pushes the tape in, but the tape won't go.

The tape won't go because there is already a tape in the VCR. Sarah sighs and hits eject and removes the tape. The tape has a faded lavender sticker that reads, in swirly starred script, *Mystical Horse Camp for Girls: Promo Video.*

She reinserts the video and hits play.

On the video are the following:

- Girls in one-piece swimsuits running in place on a log in a lake with pine trees all around them like it's pioneer times.
- A girl with teeny bangs and rounded cheer shorts attentively brushing a horse's doll-hair tail.

- The horse itself, all muscle and curve and guarded-but-needy eyes.
- The horse's face, bumping faces with the attentively brushing girl's face like they are BFFs.
- Lots of girls with their arms around each other, swaying and falling and laughing in the pines.
- A girl with boy-short hair in a giant inflatable hamster wheel in a lake, arms and legs flapping and flapping as the blow-up circle rolls.

The video is old, Sarah can see. The fashions are outdated (which Sarah thinks is awesome). The picture looks fuzzed. This place might not even exist and Sarah knows this, but it's still impossible for Sarah not to hope that horse camp is part of her twelfth birthday gift, is the real present.

RESPONDING TO THE CALL

When Sarah goes down for dinner, she asks her mom whether horse camp is part of her present. She asks it nonchalantly, not wanting to reveal the intensity of her desire. "Horse camp?" her mom kind of shouts as she opens a paper container of Chinese food. She is shouting at no one so no one answers. "Here," she says. "I got that broccoli you like."

Sarah imagines herself curled on a hay bed in a stable, sleeping in the dank dark lulled by fur and heaving beast breath. She imagines it with that sentence, which sounds romantic. Sarah imagines herself giving BFF nuzzles to her horse's horseface.

Sarah cuts her bangs and asks her mom for cheer shorts.

Sarah wears the cheer shorts in her room at night and yells *SOMEONE SAVE ME, SOMEONE TAKE ME AWAY FROM THIS AWFUL PLACE!* When she yells this she becomes Sarah from *Labyrinth*, but David Bowie does not show up at her window to take her to horse camp. The oversized vest and poet's blouse she is now wearing look weird with the cheer shorts.

CROSSING THE THRESHOLD TO THE SPECIAL WORLD

Years pass. Sarah is still Sarah from *Labyrinth* and still twelve. She still waits for David Bowie.

But instead of being carried away by David Bowie or finding a portal, Sarah is driven by her mom to college at a Big Ten school. This will have to be the special world.

The whole way there, Sarah wears her vest and cheer shorts in case she sees it, sees horse camp the way Susan Walker sees her dream house paid-for and empty on 34th Street and *knows*. STOP, she will yell. STOP THE CAR.

At the Big Ten school, Sarah's mom takes her to Bed Bath & Beyond. She buys her a bunch of stuff from the college dorm aisle: T-shirt sheets, pillows, a stack of plastic drawers, a little rug, a shower caddy. At Sarah's dorm, Sarah's mom organizes everything herself. "Sar, I got you all the same white socks so you don't have to worry about pairing them up," she said, ripping open the plastic with her acrylic nails and stuffing socks in the clear drawer. "You can throw them out after you wear them because I know you're not real good at keeping them clean. I'll just send you a package of socks every month, okay?"

Sarah signs up for English and Spanish, which are required, plus Zoology and Eastern European history. Sarah thinks it's important to understand how someone's biology works if you're going to be their BFF, important to know how their systems affect their emotions, et cetera, especially if they can't talk. And she wants to learn about horses' place of origin, to know what kinds of stories and struggles might live way deep inside them.

TESTS, ALLIES, AND ENEMIES

Even though Sarah is twelve, she has always been school-smart, which is what people say to Sarah when they find out her test scores: "Oh, so you're *school-smart*." The other kind of smart is called street-smart, which Sarah gets they're implying she is *not*. Sarah is street-smart enough, though, to know that street-smart is the kind that matters. Because she is not street-smart, but is a good student, she begins to study and then mimic the behavior of the other kids in the dorm.

For example: everyone in Sarah's dorm lipsticks the school's initials on their cheeks for football games and drinks beer that tastes like throw-up, so Sarah does, too.

For example: everyone in Sarah's dorm rushes a fraternity or a sorority, so Sarah does, too.

An all-girl mansion sounds nice, anyway, even if there aren't any horses.

TEST 1: at the sorority house, Sarah is forced to stay up all night memorizing the lyrics to all of the sorority's songs. It is the night before her Zoology midterm and she keeps saying "I have a Zoology midterm!" but none of her Sisters respond at all.

So instead of learning about the Krebs cycle, which will help her become a good BFF for a horse and eventually help her build a time machine, Sarah is chanting "Down with virginity, up with the vice! Now that you've got me on the ground, I might as well give you a slice!" Sarah doesn't really understand these lyrics. She wonders about "a slice." A slice of what? Sarah is not street-smart. But then she thinks about her body on the ground, and she knows what the slice part is.

Every part of Sarah wants to go back to her dorm and learn about the Krebs cycle. But Sarah is twelve and doesn't know how to put an end to things that aren't going well.

Sarah wishes she could be not-twelve, but she has an age disorder.

Sarah moves into the sorority house.

Sarah has failed test 1.

TEST 2: one day there is a party. Everyone spends a lot of time getting ready. "Do you think I'm wearing too many shades of tan?" Sarah's roommate asks her. Sarah doesn't know. Sarah senses there are a lot of rules here, but she doesn't know what they are and wishes the rules were just posted somewhere so that she could memorize how many shades of tan were too many, etc.

At the party, the floor is covered in a very sticky layer and the room smells eggy and everyone is drinking alcoholic juice that tastes like bug juice from day camp plus cleaning solution. The juice is scooped with plastic cups from a lined garbage can, which Sarah thinks is more upsetting than an unlined one. Sarah stands around near some of her Sisters sort of bobbing her head to the music as she drinks juice from the garbage can. A Frat Boy asks Sarah if she wants a refill and Sarah has drunk all her bug juice and the boy is cute so she says yes. Sarah and the boy are drinking and bobbing their heads to the music, which is too loud to hear anything else. "Wanna go upstairs where it's quieter? I'd love to be able to talk more!"

Sarah nods enthusiastically.

Upstairs where it's quieter is a boy room with two twin beds and two desks with boxy computers on them and a futon. Sheets are peeling off the bed's mattress. Sarah and the Frat Boy sit on the futon, which is leaking foam a little from the corner. Sarah likes this room, likes the *college boy*-ness of it. She is intrigued by college boys, as a concept. She likes the way they walk, their voices, their hands. She'd imagined more glasses, more philosophical pontification, but this is okay, too.

"So what's your major?" the Frat Boy asks.

"I'm taking Zoology and Eastern European History right now," Sarah says. "I guess I want to study horses." The Frat Boy is the first person who she's told this to so directly. There is something about his focus on her, his deep-set eyes, his long fingers wrapped around his red Solo cup, that make her want to make herself visible.

"Horses, that's so cool," says the Frat Boy, lifting Sarah's chin and kissing her. Sarah is excited to be kissed; she has always wanted to be kissed! and this Frat Boy is cute. The kiss has happened faster than Sarah imagined, but she knows that that's because this boy must see how special she is, how beautiful, how loving of horses. Because he must feel an instant connection. Sarah feels one, too.

Then, Frat Boy starts vigorously rubbing the crotch area of

Sarah's jeans. Sarah has really wanted to be touched here by a boy, but this isn't how she imagined it. The touch feels like hard, weird pawing and the seams of Sarah's jeans are rough and sort of hurt. She sort of wants to leave, or to try to reinhabit the magic of the moment before, but she doesn't know how to do either. She thinks of the song: "Now that you've got me down on the ground..." She understands this is a rule now, a hidden one, that the rules aren't going to be posted, but they'll be taught to her anyway. She is down on a futon, not the ground, but she gets that it still counts. The Frat Boy shoves his hand in Sarah's mouth and she sees now that the slice thing doesn't necessarily refer to a specific body part, that it was metonymic. That's a word Sarah learned in English. Sarah sees that she is being taught everything she needs to know. Sarah's mouth opens.

Sarah has failed this test.

TEST 3 is Sarah's Zoology test. She fails that, too.

UNCROSSING THE THRESHOLD

Sarah is back on the other side of the threshold. Her journey feels derailed. She is in the Ordinary World.

It is Christmas break and Sarah is lying on her bed looking at the small pink TV with the built-in VCR and Sarah feels like, this sorority life cannot be her life. She feels like, how did she become this Sarah, a Sarah who is answering questions about numbers of shades of tan instead of answering questions about the Krebs cycle. Something, she knows, needs to change.

Sarah puts her cheer shorts on and waits on the steps of

her old high school's main building for an unassuming middle-aged man in a suit to approach her and say, *You must come with me. Your destiny awaits.* This is what would feel obvious and right. This does not happen, but she does become Buffy Summers, whose real name is also Sarah, since, Sarah knows, Sarah Michelle Gellar and Buffy Summers are one and the very same person.

REFUSAL OF THE CALL

When Sarah returns to the sorority house, her Sisters have turned into plastic doll versions of themselves. It's hard to see—they look almost the same as before—but one of Sarah's sisters is wearing a tube top, and Sarah can clearly see that this sister's arms are hinged mechanically onto her body. This isn't the plot of any actual *Buffy* episode, but Sarah sees how it could be one.

The dolls freeze, posed, in the hallway and stare at Sarah.

"Can I look through your closet, Sarah?" one doll lilts. "I'm going to a skank-themed party and I bet you have something perfect."

This doll's friend is linked arm-in-plastic arm with her, and is pretending to try to hold back her laughter. This doll says in a pull-string voice: "I think Sarah's stuff will be too big for us."

A third doll approaches and goes, "Let's teach Sarah to make herself puke!" She grabs Sarah's hair and yanks, forcing Sarah's head back, and a fourth doll shoves the four glued-together fingers of her hand into Sarah's mouth, followed by her entire plastic wrist.

Sarah cries out, a gurgle.

"We're helping you!" a pull-string voice shouts back.

Sarah tears off the arm of the assaulting doll at the shoulder, which enables her to remove it from her own throat. Sarah swings the arm like a bat, bashing it straight into the head of the first doll who approached. It punctures the plastic head, which releases a hissing stream of air. All the other dolls run.

Sarah gets kicked out of the sorority.

MEETING WITH A MENTOR

Joyce Summers, Buffy's TV mom, drives up to help Sarah move. Joyce is pretty supportive. This is just like when Buffy got kicked out of high school. She doesn't understand why these things happen to her sweet daughter, but she understands they aren't entirely her fault. Joyce helps Sarah find a studio apartment downtown. "I think being downtown will give you a chance to meet other kinds of people," Joyce says. "But also you'll have some space to yourself to figure out what you love, what kinds of people are right for you."

This advice is astoundingly different from anything the mom Sarah grew up with might say. The mom Sarah grew up with would say that if she wasn't liking it here, she should just come back home already.

The apartment Joyce helps Sarah find is up a beer-and-sweat-smelling staircase. It has big windows and scuffed wooden floors and below it is a coffee shop full of girls with pastel hair and long gauzy dresses and Doc Martens or else buzz cuts and striped mock-neck shirts and glasses.

After Joyce leaves, Sarah decides to take Joyce's advice about figuring out what she loves and spending time alone. She takes a bunch of psychology classes because she needs to be a BFF to herself. She hopes the psych classes will help her figure out why she can't stop being twelve when everyone else seems to get older.

She goes to the coffee shop a lot and reads her psychology books.

One day she notices that there is a group of three girls who've been staring at her. The girls seem eerily close to each other, and they are all wearing identical black schoolgirl skirts, styled in different ways. Sarah feels her mouth opening and her arms crossing in front of her. Her heart speeds up and she doesn't know why yet.

But then one girl approaches. Short messy hair, chokers and chains, intense burgundy lipstick. "Hey, I'm Nancy," the girl says. "Wanna come sit with us?"

Sarah sees what is happening.

She turns into Sarah from *The Craft*.

TEST, ALLIES, ENEMIES—AGAIN

TEST 1: Sarah goes to sit with Nancy and the other witches. As they introduce themselves and their roles in the coven, Nancy is looking at Sarah like she is assessing her, but not like she is thinking about how many calories are in Sarah's latte, whether it is skim or soy. Nancy's mouth is sort of opening and closing. Sarah has of course heard of lesbians, but she has never met one. She gets very suddenly that Nancy is a lesbian.

"Why are you here by yourself so much?" one of the girls asks. "We always see you here."

Sarah tells her that she's recently moved to the apartment above the café, that she comes here to study.

"You live alone?" Nancy says, "That's so cool. Can I come up and sage your new place?"

"Sure," says Sarah, nervous. No one but Joyce Summers has ever been over.

Leaving the café, Sarah fantasizes about running into one of her former sorority Sisters, about having them see her on the street with this girl with choppy hair and terrifying burgundy lips.

At Sarah's apartment, Nancy picks up a marble horse figurine. "Horses represent raw sexual energy," Nancy says. "That's why little girls are all horse-obsessed." Nancy smirks as she sets the horse down. "Little boys are allowed to be obsessed with girls, and little girls are allowed to be obsessed with horses." Sarah is carrying two glasses of Lipton powder mixed with water and her hands feel stuck around the glasses. Nancy removes the glasses from Sarah's hands, one at a time, and sets them down on the fake wood credenza. "Let's do a spell."

Nancy goes and collects ginger from the kitchen, a fake feather from a boa, some seashells, and a candle. Then she sits cross-legged in front of Sarah, almost knee-to-knee. Not a single part of their bodies is touching but Sarah can feel the tenseness of their bodies very intensely.

"Let's use our combined energy to try to make the horse figurine fly," Nancy says.

"Okay," says Sarah.

Sarah's eyes bore into Nancy's eyes, and she can feel the

vibrations between them, this quick and tense energy. She knows what to do. Sarah uses her pointer finger to direct the energy toward the horse figurine, to push it off the table and lift it up.

Nancy starts screaming. "You're amazing!" She is screaming "You're amazing!" She is saying all kinds of stuff to Sarah, like she had this feeling about Sarah, like Sarah is a real witch.

Then Sarah and Nancy are kissing and Sarah pays close attention to Nancy as this is happening, to the way Nancy's lips express what she wants so precisely. Nancy wants to devour Sarah with her terrifying burgundy mouth, which is suddenly filled with teeth. That's okay, Sarah thinks.

Soon Nancy is naked and Sarah is naked and Sarah feels she is being devoured, and somehow Nancy's entire hand is inside Sarah's body, and so Sarah feels she is devouring, too, feels that her body can pull Nancy in, can digest her. They are both making gurgles and scream sounds that Sarah did not know the human body could make, but then she realizes they are like birthing sounds and then Sarah and Nancy are draped over each other and breathing hard.

Sarah feels destroyed and remade. Sarah sees that what she has is not a slice at all but a kind of meaty machine that can eat and expel and transfigure.

Sarah has passed this test.

TEST 2: Sarah has never met any lesbians and so she doesn't know any lesbian jokes and so she lets Nancy move in.

Sarah is obsessed with thinking about: *am I a lesbian now?* It seems like the kind of thing you should have already known about, not the kind of thing you just find yourself being. Nancy shows Sarah *Gia* and *High Art* and *The L Word*. Sarah starts wearing corduroys and big navy sweaters. She cuts her hair to ear-length.

Sarah and Nancy light candles and cook whole vegetables and apply winged liquid eyeliner and smoke cloves in the street and watch movies and buy amulets and dye their hair different colors and do tarot readings and decorate their apartment and wear each other's clothes. They make a world that is all crystal and gauze and hair dye and tarot and it is a good world.

Sarah has passed this test.

APOTHEOSIS

But then Nancy starts getting annoyed with Sarah. She yells at Sarah for getting zucchini all over the kitchen every time she makes stir-fry, for refusing to put a curse on Nancy's asshole TA, for bursting into tears all the time for absolutely no reason.

But there is a reason: Sarah is twelve.

Sarah has no friends. She doesn't know where horse camp is and she can't even major in physics anymore. Sarah needs a mommy or else a horse. She wants Nancy to be both mommy and horse and also BFF and sister and daddy and self. Nancy can't be all these things and Sarah is so sad about that. She cries and cries.

Sarah looks in the mirror and sees that who she has become is Sarah Schuster, the fictional alter ego of Jenny from *The L Word*. It is really hard being Sarah Schuster. She experiences near-constant flashbacks of her empty-feeling childhood, of her thwarted desire for horse camp, of doll arms and boy hands entering her throat against her will.

Sarah cries, so Nancy yells; Nancy yells, so Sarah cries. When Nancy yells, she is vicious, baring her teeth and getting crazy-faced and sometimes throwing things. When Sarah cries, she heaves and wails, sounding like a baboon or a train, but more pathetic. When Sarah cries, she makes little cuts in her upper arm with the kitchen knife and watches the blood bloom and run. Forcing Nancy to watch the blood seep makes her feel like she's allowing Nancy to witness the degree of her pain, and she doesn't know why, but she likes this.

"I'm leaving," Nancy announces one day. "I'm moving to Austin to do AmeriCorps."

Sarah heaves and wails. She makes many animal sounds and soaks her face from every orifice. Sarah's face looks like a wet dark hole and she sounds like GUUUUUUUGHHHH.

"I'm leaving the number for a suicide hotline on the fridge," Nancy yells across the room.

But Sarah doesn't use the number for the suicide hotline.

Instead, Sarah kills herself.

ORDEAL

When Sarah wakes up from being dead, she looks at her face in the mirror and it is the face of someone who is not twelve, the face of an unrecognizable Sarah. This Sarah has small bags under her eyes and her tits have loosened. She is like twenty-eight, she thinks. There is only one crystal left in the apartment, a clear quartz. She holds it in her hand and realizes, there is no horse camp. Why has it taken Sarah so long to realize horse camp doesn't exist? Sarah has never been street-smart.

APPROACH TO THE INNERMOST CAVE

There's a student loan check in Sarah's mailbox. Sarah cashes it, buys an old Honda for $1,500, and decides to drive across the country. Before she goes, though, she cuts off all her hair with the kitchen scissors, leaving it in piles on the floor. She finds a tube of thick and reflective red gloss and uses it to fully lacquer her lips. Sarah is going to move to a real city, not this Big Ten nightmare camp. She doesn't know who she will be there, but she's excited to find out.

Sarah doesn't bring any clothes. She is going to need new clothes.

REWARD

Sarah goes through the north part of the country, driving through the North Woods of Minnesota and Wisconsin. The trees of the North Woods are her favorite trees, Sarah decides. They don't seem intent on expressing their own spectacularness, they seem happy to work together in creating leafy walls, in releasing oxygen, et cetera.

She stops in Duluth and goes to a Friday fish fry, she stops in Minneapolis and eats pierogies, she stops to swim in a lake. At the lake, Sarah floats in Hanes bikini briefs and a tank top, plus her new close-cropped hair and red lips. The water is so, so cold. She mermaid swims underwater, and then flips sideways, splashing back. She feels like she could spend her whole life this way, a water creature. She floats on her back and spreads her limbs out star-style, feeling the sun on her face.

She returns to her Motel 6 room to change. She loves the anonymity of the room, the feeling of distance, like she's floating far away from everyone she's ever known, like she could incubate here, become anything.

She's hungry so she wanders down a street to look for food and ends up in a thrift store. She leafs through floral prints and plaids in the women's section and, feeling uninspired by them, wanders over to the men's. She spins a round rack of denim vests and then tries one on, kind of boxy, kind of frayed. She gets a glimpse of herself and loves how she looks. Why had she always relegated herself to one half of the store?

Wearing her new vest, Sarah continues down the street. She sees a store with a fat mermaid on its sign and a tote bag that says *Mother Nature is a Lesbian* in its window, plus books with titles like *Sister Outsider, Teaching to Transgress, Cunt Coloring Book*. She feels drawn to the store, seeing all these things in one place, like the store is full of answers to questions she didn't know she had. Inside, there are whole sections on lesbian herstory, queer theory, international women's movements, domestic abuse, racialized violence, psychology, self-help, plants. There are crystals and menstrual cups and stickers. After spending an hour leafing through books, Sarah chooses a road map of queer businesses throughout the U.S., a guide to native plants, and an academic text analyzing cultural representations of girls and horses from a psychoanalytic perspective. The person behind the counter is skinny with a lavender mane of hair, tattoos that look like someone's bored drawings, and a single thick triangle earring. "I was a horse kid, too," they say. It feels cool to hear them say this, like there are secret horse kids interspersed throughout the population of the world, like being a horse kid meant something.

Sarah wanders into a vegan diner and gets fried soy chicken and curly fries. She sits in a sparkly booth with her books spread around her and looks up queer spaces slightly west of where she is. She reads about a Chinese restaurant in North Dakota that, since the '70s, transforms into a drag club at night. She gets out her map and plans her route to North Dakota, imagines showing up in boy drag to eat noodles and watch queens sing and, maybe, meet all the queer people from miles around. She gets out her plant book to see what plants she can find in North Dakota: wild garlic, cattail, maidenhair fern, whorled milkweed.

RESURRECTION

The next morning, Sarah picks up a coffee and drives west. She streams a mix of music she got from Nancy, music the sorority girls liked, and music she Shazamed at the bookstore. "*STAND-ING IN THE WAY OF CONTROL! YOU LIVE YOUR LIFE!*" screams Beth Ditto, and Sarah screams it, too.

And then, suddenly, Sarah feels it. *STOP!* a voice in her brain says. *Stop the car!*

Sarah obeys the voice. She pulls over and leaps out of the passenger seat, leaving the door wide open. Her legs feel unaffected by gravity, buoyant, hyperspeed as she runs into the trees.

The forest floor is mulchy but Sarah is compelled onward, twigs cracking beneath her feet until she feels the airspot that is a door, until she is sucked through the airspot, until there are horses, curvy and muscled and maned.

RETURN WITH THE ELIXIR

Sarah looks at the horses tossing their gorgeous horse heads. She meets the eyes of the horse that looks most trustworthy and it blinks at her, looks for just a moment at her as though it is *really looking*, and then nuzzles its face against Sarah's face with the gentlest BFF nuzzle ever. Sarah lets herself fully feel the nuzzle, and then Sarah says, "I'll be right back."

The horse seems to understand. It looks at Sarah like it's been waiting awhile and whatever right back means is okay. In the distance, Sarah sees a row of cheer shorts.

Sarah reenters the portal, lands in the forest, makes a mental note of the three fused trees growing right next to the portal. She knows she won't be right back, depending on what right back means, but that she wants to see a drag show in North Dakota, to know what it is to pull wild garlic out of the earth. Sarah gazes back though, for when she's ready. She tries to memorize the exact look of the horizon, to mentally record the shape of the trees.

THE PURPLE EPOCH

Sarah is dead and so are all the other Sarahs. The ocean is green and chunks of still-existing land are covered with cockroaches, who survive everything. The cockroaches cavort in burnt metal shells and on plains of melted plastic. Everything else is scorched and dead. Hollowed out clownfish stick and dry on the femurs of former Sarahs.

Their bones would look the same, if anyone was there to see them—dolphin scientists and dungeon Mistresses, sad girl poets and trophy wives, oil drillers and onion harvesters have become piles of ivory sticks, tumbled smooth like driftwood by the radioactive sea.

The sea is putrid and foamy. Styrofoam bobs everywhere in tiny popcorn pieces and great slabs swathed in algal goo. The coral is bleached white and disintegrated, floating in pieces that at first glance look indistinguishable from the Styrofoam, indistinguishable from the bones. Under layers of oil and toxic waste, pale and glowing fish with balloon heads and dragon tails survive. They look like dancing spinal cords and movie ghosts as they navigate the two feet of liquid remaining beneath the oil.

Eventually, it gets them: the iridescent blue-lipped fishies are trapped in coagulated gasoline.

Meanwhile, winds and heat and other forces break the bones of the Sarahs apart. The bones become shards and then sand. The sand that was bones stays dry and loose and turns into beaches. The sand that was bones gets wet with bacteria-filled water and turns into bluffs overlooking the toxic, glowing sea.

The earth enters a purple epoch. The sea is purple and covers almost everything. New bacteria take reign during the purple epoch. The hotter temperatures create a party atmosphere for all kinds of sporrias and phillas and cocci. Flava and pusilla and humiferous bloom and spew, knitting together in great roiling clouds. The ocean fills with jellies and foams and thick mists formed by strange combinations of violaceum and plastic, of globiformus and tin. Bacteria are born who love the plastic, who gobble it like a snack and become part plastic. Bacteria are born who love the plastic in a different way, who help it join together in great multicolored reefs. There are waves and more waves, and the bacteria and materials get bored of each other and the ocean becomes all liquidy again, clear purple.

The continents disappear in the deluge and millions of years or two seconds later, they emerge. They move around a little and new chunks of land break off.

Plastic and Styrofoam and tin have glommed together in the temperate region that was once the arctic and formed a new continent. This continent is shiny and beautiful, with metal spires, with reflective plastic flats, with bumpy white hills of transformed foam. The transformed foam is so nice—imagine Styrofoam adhered together in clumps that've been kilned and shellacked: it looks like that.

Bacteria smush their genes around and make bigger bacteria and then slimy ocean swimmers and then tentacled ones and then rooted green and purple streamerlike ones. The swimmers get bigger and leggier. They develop better vision and more elaborate ways of loving each other. They rub up and combine in ways that eventually lead to underwater breathing and easily manipulatable fingerlike extensions. They climb out of the sea, onto the continent of foam spires and plastic slides and multi-textured mountains. They've been created in this world and so this world feels exactly right. The radioactive air feels perfect. Their already-reptilian skins thrive, getting the vitamins they crave when they lie chest-up directly under the missing ozone.

Because they have come from the sea, the creatures are good at controlling their breathing, and so they can make very specific sounds and after a couple million years, the specific sounds come to mean things.

The creatures find bones and put them together. They do this accurately to make erect humans and whales and they do this inaccurately and put a dolphin head on a human body. They make an accidental centaur. From these misassembled bones, new mythologies emerge, of what the world was before.

The creatures get names. No one is ever named Sarah again, but one day a creature is called something like Sah-wah.

Sah-wah walks on the talon-ends of six jointed legs through a white tunnel made of former plastics and foams, though to it, the tunnel just feels organic, calming. In an iridescent crack in the rock, Sah-wah sees a perfectly preserved glass prism, the kind that used to hang in hippie apartments, reflecting rainbows all over the tunnel. It feels full of praise and love for something that doesn't have a name. Sah-wah sees a tiny square rainbow on the rough lavender-gray skin of one of its legs and feels a surge of connection to something from another world, something that feels far in the future, or the past. It watches the rainbow expand on the shining white wall in front of it and feels so grounded, so alive, so home.

ACKNOWLEDGMENTS

So much gratitude to:

The editors who published these stories individually—Andrea Lawlor at *Fence*, Raluca Albu at *Bomb*, Gina Abelkop at the wonderful queer and feminist Birds of Lace Press.

My agent, Meredith Kaffel Simonoff, whose depth of vision, fierce advocacy, and generosity of heart and spirit make me want to cry just thinking about it.

My editor, Maddie Caldwell, who I knew from the get had all the requisite brilliance and weirdness to co-create a world of Sarahs. Thank you for your clarity and commitment, for pushing hard to make this book the best version of itself.

Jacqueline Young, Anjuli Johnson, Tree Abraham, Jordan Rubinstein, Alana Spendley, and the rest of the team at Grand Central Publishing for thoughtful work to help this book find its way.

The PhD Creative Writing program at the University of Southern California for years of miraculous-feeling support, with a special thank-you to my teachers there: Aimee Bender, Dana Johnson, and Maggie Nelson.

MacDowell for allowing me to finish this book in an enchanted forest of old frozen trees and genius babe artists.

Karen Tongson for fierce commitment to helping me "Don Draper this shit." Jean Chen Ho for setting me up with my agent. Emily Geminder, Raquel Gutierrez, and Chris Belcher for reading drafts of stories and offering feedback.

Nikki Darling for believing in my writing so consistently for so long that I haven't had to. Gina Abelkop for days-long slumber parties in which I've become my writer-self and my self-self. Sandra Rosales for keeping my head straight and my face clean, for wanting to be a tree, whose support has made so much possible.

Lezerati for being such a generous and generative place to bring work: thank you, Adrienne Walser, Alicia Vogl Saenz, Jane Ward, Judith Branzburg, Lynn Ballen, Robin Podolosky.

Asher Hartman and Amanda Yates-Garcia for helping me connect to the spirits. Julie Tolentino for letting me write in your magic desert house. Laurie Weeks for teaching me to approach writing with my whole body and being.

CalArts, and everyone on the writing faculty there, for setting me off in search of weirdness and innovation, always.

My parents, Marvin Cohen and Karen Tessler, for their constant, wild support. My brother, Brad Cohen, who teaches me to find the humor in all things.

Ilene Adler for being a perpetual grounding force. The Sklar family, who made me the family storyteller. Shelia Solomon, Barbara Cohen, Ron Cohen, Karen Fink, and Ruthie Koczlowski for showing me art and helping me grow up.

ACKNOWLEDGMENTS

For conversation, for creating space to imagine otherwise, for feeding and holding me in so many ways, at different points: Alison Picard, Amanda Ackerman, Amanda-Faye Jimenez, Brandi Wells, Carol Cheh, Colin Fleming, Corinna Widhalm, Daviel Shy, Gabriella Burnham, Isabelle Basher, Iván Ramos, JD Scott, K Leenhouts, Kyunghee Sabina Eo, Laura Been, Martabel Wasserman, Maryam Hosseinzadeh, Megan Milks, Parisa Parnian, Saehee Cho, Sara Gerot, Sarah Kessler, Sol Alvarez, Stephen van Dyck, Tricia Maharaj, and Wei Tchou.

Goose and Carly for keeping me wild.